FIRST LIGHT

FIRST LIGHT

RED RAIN #5.5

RACHEL NEWHOUSE

rachelnewhouse.com

JUNE 2076
PRESENT DAY

1

It was the fourth time she'd died this week.

She'd died every night since Sunday. Only Wednesday night had spared her, but that was due to my self-imposed insomnia and not any luck on her part.

Now it was Thursday night—or, more accurately, the inhumanely early hours of Friday morning—and I knew as soon my head hit the pillow that she would not live to see daylight.

There was no variety to the murders, which irked me. In another life, my subconscious had been more creative in inflicting punishment, but apparently I was losing my touch.

Every night was the same. It started with the smell—the burning stench of rusted metal that seared my nostrils. Then there was the clanging of decapitated machines, the wailing of unhelpful sirens, and the swaying of the broken platform as it bucked beneath my feet.

And then, before I could even orient myself and regain control of my muscles, she fell.

Sometimes she screamed. Sometimes she was silent. Sometimes, when I was feeling particularly self-loathing, she called my name. But each time, she hung eerily mid-air, her descent slowing until I fooled myself into thinking I could reach her in time.

But I never did. Every time the world restarted, and every time she dropped like a rock. And in this reality, there was nothing to break her fall.

Tonight, I didn't even try to save her. I walked to the edge of the platform and gripped the railing, ignoring the burn of Red Rain on my fingers. I watched her fall, her dark hair rippling in slow-motion like she was floating in a river, and willed her to die. I wished she would hit the ground so I could wake up.

And then, suddenly, I did.

I shattered into reality. A shrill ring pierced my ears; I glanced at the tablet on my bedside table and realized someone was calling me. Normally I would have cursed the intrusion, but this time, it could not have been more opportune. I took a deep breath, relishing the darkness of the room, and toyed with the idea of being grateful.

Then I noticed the caller ID and remembered I had absolutely nothing to be thankful for.

I sat up and grabbed the device. She'd only called me once since she left. And while there had been a very valid reason for that call, she *should* have been calling me every day. I was the only responsible adult in her life, despite what her father might say, and she needed me.

But she was too stubborn to ask for help, and I was too stubborn to point that out, so we'd barely talked since she left. Which meant, if she was motivated enough to call me, it could only be bad news.

My nightmares weren't over. They were about to become reality.

I rubbed my temples even as I accepted the call. I didn't have the emotional energy for any of the pedestrian chatter she might use to try and frame her confession, so as soon as the line picked up, I declared:

"Who died?"

My prophetic accuracy stunned her long enough for me to flip on a light and stumble over to the coffee maker I had on my dresser for just such emergencies.

"Uh... what?" she finally managed.

I sighed and tossed the tablet on the dresser. One of these days she would realize that I knew a lot more than she gave me credit for, but today was not that day. "It's the middle of the night over here." I walked her through it as I fumbled with the safety seal on a coffee pod. "So either you forgot to look up interplanetary time zones, or someone's dead."

She was silent, and I had my answer. It would be nice to be wrong once in a while.

"Well," she hesitated, as she always did when she was guilty, "no one's dead yet..."

Oh, how my sanity swings on that operative word. I jammed the pod in the machine and punched the button. If only the relative force would make the relief brew faster.

"...that's why I need your help."

My inner tirade derailed as her words flooded me with an emotion that was entirely inappropriate for the situation.

By way of invitation, I softened my tone. "What happened?"

She didn't take me up on my offer. She went silent again.

Before I could repeat myself using more affirmative language, another voice inserted themselves into the conversation. "I can explain if you want."

"Who's that?" I snapped. My muscles immediately went on the defensive, although I think it had more to do with the fact that the voice was distinctly young and male than with the fact that I couldn't place him.

"Stanyard," she answered, and then rudely made me figure it out for myself.

Memories of the dark-haired bundle of angsty hormones came into focus, and I became even more confused. "The kid?" I coughed. She could do so much better.

"Wow, specific," he muttered.

I was more than happy to remind him of his claim to fame. "The one who abandoned you in an alley—"

"Yes, yes," she cut me off in a fluster, which confirmed my suspicions. "Ephesus is here too."

Logically, I knew that her brother being with her was an improvement of her situation, if only a marginal one. But the fact that they'd miraculously reunited overnight—when a mere twelve hours ago she'd had no idea where he was—told me that she had not been laying low like she promised.

Suddenly, there were a lot of words I wanted to say. But I opted not to waste my breath on them and instead just swore.

Ephesus returned the sentiment from somewhere in the background.

I abandoned my coffee and strode back to the desk. "Well, this ought to be an excellent bedtime story." I flicked my monitor on and pulled up a note file. "Start from the beginning, Andromeda."

She hesitated again. I contemplated threatening her with her real name but decided I'd better not forfeit my ace so early in the conversation. Instead, I settled on, "And if you were thinking of holding anything back, let me remind you that this app encrypts calls."

She mumbled her defeat. "You said it wasn't bulletproof..."

"It's a risk I'm willing to take," I announced, and hoped she would appreciate the sacrifice. "Start talking."

She finally obeyed me, and that was where the warm fuzzy feeling ended.

Her story was a nightmare, worse than any I'd been concocting lately. She'd blown her cover; her dad had been cryogenically frozen; and my former assistant had nearly murdered her. It was a trainwreck of one ghastly mistake after another, and unfortunately for all involved, she could not be blamed for all of it.

I was used to a baseline of idiocy from her. I knew how to do damage control on her stupidity. But I hadn't planned on being slapped in the face with my own.

"Carnegie must have picked him up outside of Andes's," she confessed, and waited for me to put the nail in the coffin.

I did so without thinking. "Oh, I'm quite sure that's exactly what happened," I snapped. I hadn't intended to vocalize my frustration, but it was preferrable to the physical demonstration I was considering.

As usual, she pitifully assumed all anger in the room was directed at her. "I know, I'm sorry, I should have—"

There were a million ways to autofill that sentence, and I regrettably chose the least helpful option. "You should have waited to contact Andes until you had your father with you, like I *told* you to!"

Would that have averted disaster? If anything, Carnegie might have just gotten two birds with one stone, and I would have handed them to him. I was the one who referred Philadelphia to Andes. If I'd remembered my manners, I would have sent her with gift wrap and a bow.

She continued to blunder through her tale, but I mentally minimized the window and devoted my processing power to berating myself. Of course Carnegie knew about Andes. He had been there the last time I had contracted Andes's services, hovering at my elbow like the wraith that he was. I hadn't thought a thing of it because he had been my assistant, a fixture of the room more than a human being.

I got up to retrieve my coffee, not that I expected it to do any good. It would take something much stronger than caffeine to dull my mood at this point. As usual, my dreams had been prophetic in more ways than one. I was too late to prevent her from crashing.

And, yet again, it was my fault that she fell.

I returned to the desk only to realize that she'd finished her story and was waiting for a response. The window to apologize had passed five minutes ago, so I decided not to make it awkward and continued with damage control. I plied her for the morbid details about her father and helped her plan her next move. I plastered on some sarcasm in an attempt to make my advice easier to swallow, but slapping lipstick on a pig would have been a more profitable endeavor. Neither of us was in any way comforted by my emotional disinterest. I was grateful when she gave me an out to end the call.

I shoved my chair back, grabbed my now-cold coffee, and strode from the room. It was well past midnight, and the base was in power-saving mode. Keypads and fluorescents that were normally blinding had gone dark, and the lonely Martian sky above the glass dome lent little light. Only the low security lamps near the floor traced out the borders of the hallway.

I could have used my security clearance to override the lights, but I didn't need to. Unlike Phil, I could get to Wing 74 without a map.

The base grew increasingly quieter, the hum of generators and monitors fading like the breath leaving a dying man, as I neared the abandoned wing. I stepped over a roll of insulation and gingerly picked my way through the maze of construction paraphernalia. I would have preferred to demolish the entire wing rather than remodel, and it probably would have been the cheaper solution. But there was one room that I had been unable to condemn for eight years, and I was under no delusion that I'd find the courage to do so now.

I tapped the keypad to wake it up and swiped my hand over it. It was one of the few areas on base that only I could get into; even Phil didn't have access to this room yet. I stepped in, let the doors shut behind me, and waited for the silence to return.

There were no security lights or windows in this room, making it as dark as a grave—which in a way, it was. I let the utter blackness envelope me, appreciating the cold air caused by the cavernous space. Even my heavy breathing echoed oddly around the near-empty dome.

I waited until the familiarity of the space calmed my nerves, then let my mind replay the conversation with Phil. After a few more sips of coffee, my engineer's brain kicked in. I sketched out the conundrum before us, as if writing an equation on a mental whiteboard, and started searching for solutions.

But there were none; I knew that. I could solve some of her immediate concerns, of course, but like Hilbert's problems, the most critical ones had no solutions.

I leaned against the wall and closed my eyes. My nightmares seemed like a mercy now; at least my subconscious had the decency to put her out of her misery quickly.

Reality was not so kind. Her father was dead. If not literally, then effectively. But it would take her weeks, possibly months of scraping at the barrel of hope to figure that out.

And I of all people knew what a hell that was.

2054
TWENTY-TWO YEARS AGO

2

"You made this?"

It was a rhetorical question—Dad's favorite literary device—so I answered it with an eyeroll. "No, I dragged you across town to look at some other kid's project."

As usual, he ignored my wittiness. Mom always appreciated my jokes more.

We were at the observatory, where a conference room had been converted into a science fair. The room was crammed to the overflowing with homemade machines and displays, of which mine was the grand prize winner.

I watched as Dad continued to circle my device. I could tell his stone-gray eyes had switched from surprise to scrutiny. I knew he was breaking my machine down in his mind, reducing it to a mental schematic and list of parts. He folded his arms behind his back and frowned, pondering—judging.

I tested the ice. "Besides, none of the other kids are smart enough to pull this off."

It was a factual statement, but I could tell by the glare he shot in my direction that I was about to get it. "Nic, we talked about this. We should always be…"

"I know, I know." I sighed in defeat. "We should always be kind to people."

Even if they're stupid, Mom would have added.

In their defense, only two of my classmates were classifiably stupid, although over half of them were trailing behind the grade average, judging by how difficult it was for them to grasp basic algebra. But none of them were even remotely capable of building what I had created.

At first glance, it looked like a regular glass terrarium, except for the bulky environmental controls on the side. A patch of alfalfa sprouted under a grow light, irrigated by a slow drip of water. It all looked boring and ordinary—until you realized that the plant was thriving in red Martian dirt.

Getting the alfalfa to grow in the alien soil wasn't the impressive part; it had taken Sardis, my project partner, only a weekend to come up with a fertilizer blend that would feed the plant for six months with one capsule. What got us a blue ribbon was my wickedly efficient greenhouse dome and irrigation system. If my calculations were correct—and they always were—my greenhouse would require only sunlight and a conservative amount of water to grow a field of food. And for Mars, which lacked in both sunlight and water, that was a scientific breakthrough.

My dad of all people would know this. But if he was impressed, he wasn't letting it on. He tapped the glass. "Where did you get these supplies?"

"Mr. Garner donated most of the parts," I explained, referring to the owner of the nearest hardware store.

Dad's eyebrows jumped off his forehead. "He *donated* all this? How'd you convince him to do that? The parts for that temperature regulator are worth at least a couple hundred."

"I explained to him that this was an important contribution to the advancement of space colonization." I pointed at the gaudy

Garner's Gears bumper sticker that was plastered on the base of my machine. It detracted from the beauty of my device, but it was a worthy sacrifice for free parts. "And I reminded him that some very important scientists—such as yourself—would be looking at the projects."

Dad knotted his eyebrows together, like he always did when I suggested something he deemed outlandish.

I cleared my throat. "I also mowed his lawn for a month."

Dad's face erupted in a smile like a forgotten volcano. "Now *that's* ingenuity, son. See, that's what happens when you're nice to people and show them what you can do for *them*, not the other way around. Why can't you treat your classmates that way?"

I shrugged. "None of them had sheet copper."

Dad laughed. He turned back to my machine and ran a hand over the fluffy blonde mustache that stuck to his lip like a dandelion. "It's very impressive," he said finally. "I'm proud of you, son."

I grinned. "Just wait 'til it goes to nationals. I heard Dr. Chen is flying in from Beijing to judge. Maybe you'll get to meet him..."

I trailed off when I realized he was rubbing his neck the way he did when he was uncomfortable. "About that..." He sighed, and my dreams shattered. "I'm not going to make it to your competition next month."

"But why?" I exclaimed, and wondered if it was worth the energy to be mad. It was the third event he'd missed this semester.

"I have to go back to Mars," he said.

I indulged in a frustrated growl, although it was only to make him feel bad. It certainly didn't make me feel any better. "You said you weren't leaving until summer!"

He shook his head. "The schedule changed."

"So tell them no." That's what I would have done.

His head continued to shake, as if he were stuck in a perpetual motion machine. "It's not like that. I don't have a choice this time."

"Why?" I said again, and it wasn't an accusation. My father was in charge of the project; nobody could tell him what to do. There wouldn't even *be* humans on Mars without him.

"There's new laws I have to obey. It's..." Dad struggled for a moment, then gave up. "It's complicated. You'll understand when you're older."

"That's what you said about metaphysics, and I understand those just fine," I snapped.

He squinted one eye at me. "You are my son, aren't you?"

I shrugged. "That's what Mom says."

He laughed. "Then I suppose I have no one to blame but myself." He turned to study the experiment next to mine, giving himself a moment to collect his thoughts. "You know that file they ask you to sign every day at school?"

How could I forget? Every afternoon they pulled us "unassimilated" out of study hall and tried to convince us that our lives would be better if we bowed to the dumb government. Their propaganda was so terrible that it failed to be funny, and it was a waste of perfectly good research time. If it took me an extra semester to complete my first associates, it would be their fault.

"Well, the United recently passed a law that says people who haven't signed the file—like me—don't get to decide when and where they work," my dad continued. "The government has to approve all my job assignments. I can't even resign without their permission."

I snorted. That sounded like more pointless paperwork, which was exactly what our government loved. "Well, luckily for them, you don't want to quit your job."

"You're right, I don't." My dad reached down to finger the blue-tipped carnations my classmate had dyed for her copy-paste experiment. "But it does mean that if they tell me to go to Mars, I have to go."

I studied the wilting flowers. I was great at math, but this wasn't adding up. "Why can't you tell them no? You tell the government off all the time. That's why we won't sign the file."

He nodded slowly, calibrating. "Yes, I could refuse—but then I might end up in jail."

"Wouldn't be the first time."

He glanced back at me. "You want me to spend a week in jail just so I can attend your science fair?"

I glared at the floor. *Here we go with the rhetorical questions again.* Of course I didn't want my father to spend more time in solitary. But it would be nice to know that I was more important to him than some stupid government regulation.

He put his hands on my shoulders. I stiffened and refused to look up.

"Nic," he said, trying to patch the bridge, "I know you're upset. I am too. And there's a time—a lot of times—for telling the government no. But I'm not doing this project just because the government told me to. It's important to me too."

I felt the anger leave my body and tried to will it back. I knew how much my dad enjoyed his work; he often said he loved Mars more than Earth.

"And I knew that if I had a conversation with my very intelligent, very grown-up son about what was happening, he would understand why I had to leave early."

I groaned and looked at the ceiling. Why were adults always trying to use my intelligence against me? "You can't flatter your way out of this, Dad."

I heard the smile creep back into his voice. "You're a kind, caring young man, Nic."

"Not listening."

"And you have a brilliant mind."

"If I pretend to be stupid, will I get less homework?"

He brushed my chin, and I had to look him in the eye. "And as long as you don't let your brilliance outrun your kindness, you're going to go places and do great things—much more than I've ever done."

My sarcastic comeback stopped in my throat. My dad had reached the summit of human achievement. He'd appeared before officials in Washington and Beijing, and he'd built colonies on the moon and Mars. He was everything I wanted to be when I grew up.

Did he really believe I could do *more* than that?

I realized I was grinning and quickly shook my head to wipe the smile off my face, lest he think he won. I shrugged out of his grasp and stepped back. "Okay, does that mean I get to go to Mars with you?"

"Oh no, we are not playing that game." He crossed his arms, but the sparkle still danced in his eyes. "You know the rules. No interplanetary travel until you're thirteen."

I mimicked his stance. "Why? Does the United have a law about that too?"

"No, but your mother does."

I moaned. If there was one force more formidable than the United government, it was my mother's will.

Dad abandoned any pretense of looking stern. "Want to see where I'm going?"

I pinched the bridge of my nose. "Dad, I'm too old for that."

I remembered the first time Dad had left for a long-term assignment on Mars. I'd only been four or five and didn't have a good grasp of object permanence, so I'd been inconsolable. To prevent a catastrophic breakdown, Dad had set up the family telescope in the backyard and taught me how to find Mars so I would always know where he was.

Dad chuckled. "No, I mean, do you want to see the base I'm going to? I can show you live footage."

My curiosity got the better of me. "They've got a livecam set up?"

He waved his hand and started walking. "Even better."

I followed him out to the lobby of the observatory. It was close to closing time—the observatory always closed early on Mondays—and only a few visitors lingered around the gift shop. We walked past the children's planetarium and the queue for the viewing room to a door marked "Faculty Only." Dad pressed his thumb on the keypad, and it let him in with a chirp.

I tried to suppress my excitement. This was where the real science happened.

We took the elevator to the top floor, then walked all the way to the back of the building, where the hall was blocked off with construction tape. Dad ducked underneath it, and I followed.

"The dome's not quite finished yet, but she works." Dad shoved open the door at the end of the hall and ushered me inside.

I darted in and stopped—the room beyond was pitch black. Dad let the door drift shut behind us, plunging us into utter darkness. I held completely still while he fiddled with a keypad near the door.

Suddenly, a deep vibrating echoed from the walls. I braced myself, feet apart, as a deafening grind filled the room. A crack appeared in the ceiling, growing wider and wider as the panels in the dome parted. Moonlight flooded the room, revealing a brand-new telescope.

She was massive—standing almost two stories tall, even at an angle—and absolutely *gorgeous*. Her secondary mirror was at least fifteen feet wide, its honeycomb panels glinting in the muted light. An elegant lattice of titanium suspended her primary mirror high in the air like a diamond ring. The whole apparatus was cradled in a massive robotic base, making it look like a small spaceship.

Dad put his arm around my shoulder, and we stood there in silence for several minutes, admiring.

"Who funded this?" I managed when I finally found my breath.

"I did."

I gaped at him and tried to wrap my mind around how cool my dad was.

He winked. "They're going to put my name above the door, so you can tell your friends your name is on an observatory."

He strode over to the control panel and tapped the touchpad. An array of monitors brightened at his touch, and a gigantic flatscreen flickered to life above his head. "She's state of the art. Completely computer-guided, with the best atmosphere-filtering capabilities for the size. And just wait until you see how clean her image is."

"Wow," I whispered, and hoped my appreciation could be translated from that syllable.

Dad started typing rapidly. "She's not fully calibrated yet, but I know where to find Mars."

He paused, finger poised over the screen. He glanced back at me. "You want to try steering her?"

I darted to his side. "Show me."

He walked me through the basics of her controls. She was a smart machine, and within five minutes I had her where I wanted her. I savored the feeling of power beneath my fingertips as I slowly traced my hand across the touchpad. The robotics whirred in response to my command, adjusting the angle until it was just right. Dad flipped a switch, and the view appeared on the flatscreen.

There was Mars, displayed on a screen that was nearly as tall as I was, in startlingly high definition. The image was so crisp that it almost seemed three-dimensional.

Dad handed me another touchpad. I tapped and dragged the image, and to my surprise, the view zoomed in even closer. Each crater and gorge showed in sharp relief as I navigated across the planet's surface like a rover.

"This is where I'll be." Dad leaned over my shoulder to tap the screen. The image focused on the Elysium Planitia. He zoomed in further, and a small black speck appeared in the valley.

"Is that... the base?" I whispered.

He nodded.

I was about to mouth my admiration—then grunted when I realized I'd fallen for his tricks again. Despite my best efforts, it did make me feel better to know exactly where my dad was going to be.

"You sure I can't come with you?" I whined.

"Next year, I promise." He slid his arm around my shoulder again. "Who knows? Keep building greenhouses like that, and they might just give you your own base. Then I'll move in with you."

"I doubt it," I muttered, and smiled.

2058
EIGHTEEN YEARS AGO

3

"This is so cool!"

"Thanks," I said, and tried to sound genuine. I personally didn't think the data was all that interesting, but Wesley, who was two grades and several dozen IQ points behind me, was too naïve to realize he was looking at a failed experiment.

He pressed his face and hands against the side of the testing chamber, leaving a sweaty smear on the glass. Inside was a model car he had contributed to the cause of science—or, I should say, what was *left* of his model car. I'd poured a vial of acid on it, and it had dissolved the plastic casing almost instantly.

The problem was that the innards of the car were made of a different kind of plastic which wasn't reactive to the compound I had made. The miniature frame and engine sat there like a skeleton, taunting me with my inadequacies. I was trying to come up with a compound that would melt both types of plastic, but after murdering half a dozen of Wesley's cars, I was no closer to the solution.

At this rate, I was going to have to do extra chores to buy him a new set.

I turned back to the whiteboard and studied my equation. I had a theory as to what chemical I could use to perfect my compound, but Dad had refused to loan me any.

"If your equation works…" he'd said.

"When," I'd corrected, and he hadn't argued.

"That compound would be far too dangerous to have in this lab."

I'd tried to convince him that I knew how to properly handle caustic chemicals; I'd experimented with far worse in the lab at the community college back on Earth. But Dad wouldn't budge. And since we were on his Martian science station, he controlled the code to the restricted substance cabinet.

And I hadn't yet figured out how to hack that.

Surely there was another chemical I could use to the same effect. I tugged on my lip and grimaced when the scratch of stubble reminded me of another of my failed experiments.

Wesley wandered over to my workstation and admired the colorful chaos of vials and flasks. "Wanna do something else?"

"No," I grunted as I set the testing chamber to neutralize the contents, "but a mental break is, unfortunately, my best option."

He rolled his eyes. "Does the great Dr. Von Nieuwenhuyse need a nap?"

"Don't call me that." I hated when people called me by my full last name; my brain got bored and moved on to another task before they finished all the syllables. That, and it made me sound old like my dad.

"Whatever, Dr. Nic," he muttered, and I accepted the compromise. "Let's play video games."

I grimaced. I'd watched Wesley play a few times and had nearly gotten a migraine from the flashing colors and stupid storyline. "I think I'd rather do my homework."

"Haha," he droned.

I glanced back at him as I started capping my open flasks. "That wasn't sarcastic."

He flushed red. "If you don't want to play with me, just say so."

"Okay." I picked up a vial and checked the label before putting it back in the holder. "I don't want to play video games with you."

"But why not?" His voice changed to a whiny wail that grated on my ears like scraping metal. "We did what you wanted to do."

"You volunteered," I reminded him.

"Yeah, because we're friends."

I hesitated.

"Look," he said, mercifully at an appropriate decibel, "I let you use my cars for your experiment. The least you could do is let me blow you up in battle once or twice."

I glanced at the testing chamber. He had a point—and playing video games for an hour was a small price to pay for the promise of his free labor tomorrow.

"Fine," I said, hoping the monument of my sacrifice was being properly conveyed. "But I need to put these chemicals away first."

I grabbed the vial holder, and he followed me back to the supply closet. The supply closet was adjacent to the server room that processed the trillions of bytes of data collected from all the station's labs. Even the readouts from my mini demolition derby had been recorded and packaged to be sent back to the sponsors on Earth. The hum of fans and overworked motherboards filled the cramped space.

I opened a chemical cabinet and started carefully filing my vials back onto the appropriate shelves. Wesley, who was more interested in computers than science, amused himself by studying the flashing lights on the wall of servers across the room.

I was halfway done when he rudely interrupted my concentration. "Hey, what's this drive for?"

"How would I know?" I said without looking back. Computers were not my favorite thing; I involved them as little as possible in my scientific process.

"It's not connected to the mainframe."

"What?" I turned around and saw the module he was pointing at: the one on the floor in the far corner, almost hidden underneath the massive steel rack that supported the other servers.

I swallowed as I abruptly remembered that I *did* know what that server was for.

And Dad had told me to protect the contents at all costs.

I tried to play dumb. "It's not? How can you tell?"

He knelt on the floor and gestured at the wires that must have meant something to him. "It's transmitting, but it's not connected to the database. It's running off another connection."

There was a very good reason for that—so that the government couldn't trace the data, like it could with all the other information that fed through the mainframe and bounced off a United satellite.

"Maybe they've got some super-secret research going on!" He grinned over his shoulder at me.

I struggled to return the gesture. "Maybe. It's probably just something dumb like environmental controls."

"Nah, even those they monitor from Earth. Maybe I can hook it to my computer and rip the contents." He grabbed the box and dragged it towards him. The cords on the back stretched and threatened to pop—and I panicked.

"Don't!"

He stopped and looked back at me. "So you *do* know what's on here."

I froze.

"It's your dad, isn't it? He's got something going on."

Yes, and he's going to kill me when he finds out we're having this conversation.

"What is it? Secret research? Illegal experiments?"

Oh, it's illegal all right.

When he saw that I wasn't budging—let alone breathing— Wesley changed his approach. He stood up and turned to face me. "C'mon, Nic, tell me." The whine returned. "I thought we were friends. You can trust me."

"Can I?" I snapped.

"Yes! I promise I won't get you in trouble. Besides, who am I going to tell? You're the only other kid here."

I rolled the vial I had in my hand between my fingers and hesitated. He had a point, and if I alienated him by refusing to share, I'd be back to wandering the halls of the station alone while my dad was at work. Wesley wasn't brilliant, but he was always willing to hang out with me.

"C'mon, Nic," Wesley repeated. "Friends always share secrets. Don't you want to be friends?"

I searched his face. He spread his arms wide and waited.

Dad will never know the difference.

I took a deep breath and let it out in a huff. "Fine. But if my dad finds out I told you—we're both dead."

He zipped his lips and winked.

I glanced out the door to make sure the lab beyond was empty before I turned back to him and declared, "It's Bibles."

He blinked, a reaction that was wholly disproportionate to the revelation I had just shared with him. "Bibles? You mean like, Christian Bibles?"

I nodded.

He took a half step back and eyed me. "So does that mean *you're* Christian? Dude, what?"

I pulled a face. *That's what surprises you about this conversation? Not the part where I said my dad was transmitting illegal media?* "Yeah? Why do you think my dad makes me get up early on Sunday?"

He snorted. "So you, like, believe a dead guy is going to get you into paradise when you die, right?"

I groaned and glanced at the ceiling. If I had known it would lead to this moronic conversation, I wouldn't have shared my secret with him. "The whole point is that He's *not* dead, but I wouldn't expect you to appreciate that nuance."

He guffawed—doubled over and *howled* like that was the funniest thing he'd heard all week. "Dude! Are you for real right now?"

My face and neck started to burn.

He struggled to swallow another laugh. "I can't believe the great Dr. Von Nieuwenhuyse is into that kind of stuff."

I clenched my fist around the vial. "There's a world of evidence proving—"

"There's a 'world of evidence' proving you're wrong." He mimicked my tone, flicking quotes in the air, then dropped his hands and snorted. "Bro, I thought you liked science and stuff. I thought you were *smart.*"

Rage flashed through me, and I answered the call. "Smarter than you," I hissed, and punched him.

He stumbled back, more from surprise than from the force of my blow. "Hey!"

"Take it back!" I shouted. I ran at him, slamming all my weight into him with my shoulder.

He tripped on the slick metal flooring and fell backwards. His skull cracked on the ground, and he cursed with words he shouldn't have known.

I leered over him. "Take it back!"

He wiped blood off his chin and struggled to rise. "Make me."

"Gladly." I kicked him to make him stay down.

He moaned, and the look in his eyes shifted. "Dude, I—"

"Take. It. Back." I raised my fist to punch him again—then remembered I had a vial of chemicals in my other hand. A vial of very caustic chemicals.

I held it up to the light.

He was smart enough to see what was coming. He tried to back away, but I had him against the wall. "Nic, I'm sorry, I—"

"Are you?" I challenged. I tipped the vial and watched the reddish liquid slide against the tube. "Tell that to Jesus."

I yanked the cap off—just as a shout echoed from the hall.

"Nic, stop!"

I turned to see my dad barreling through the doorway. "What are you doing?"

"He's going to kill me!" Wesley squeaked, hands over his face.

"I'm not going to kill you," I snarled. "And he insulted me—and God."

Dad slowly reached out and closed his hand around my wrist. "Wesley, go to your quarters."

Wesley scrambled up. "But he—"

"I said go to your quarters," my father repeated in a way that left no room for argument. "I will talk to your father later."

Wesley growled and stormed to the door. He paused and cast one final jab at me. "You're going to regret this."

I opened my mouth, but my dad was faster. "Wesley. Now."

Wesley huffed and ran off.

"Did you hear what he said? You have to stop him!" I exclaimed.

Dad did not seem concerned by Wesley's threat. He gingerly slid the vial from my fingers and screwed the cap on. Then he twisted the tube to read the chemical contents. His eyes went wide.

"It wouldn't have killed him," I said quickly.

"No, but he might have gone blind." Dad turned and put the flask back in the cabinet, then shut the doors and keyed a code into the lock pad. My heart sank to my stomach.

When Dad turned back to me, the adrenaline had left his face, leaving his expression etched with worry. "Nic, what were you thinking?"

"He called me an idiot!" I exclaimed, all the heat of the argument rushing back to me.

"That's it?"

"No, I mean..." I struggled to hold onto my rage, but something about my dad's presence sapped it out of me. "We were talking about religion, and he said I was stupid for believing in a dead guy."

Dad's eyes searched me. "Why were you talking about religion?"

"He found out about the Bibles," I blurted, and then too late realized what I'd done.

To my surprise, Dad's face remained calm. "He 'found' out?"

"Yeah, he asked why the server wasn't connected to the mainframe, and…"

I trailed off. Dad arched one eyebrow.

I looked at the floor. "I told him."

Dad sighed, and I could hear the fear in his breath. But it was gone as quickly as it came, and when he spoke again his voice was soft, gentle—disappointed. "I'll deal with that later. But, Nic, that wasn't worth blinding him for. He could have been very seriously injured, and then what?"

And then he would have never laughed at me again.

I didn't say the words aloud, but I didn't need to. My dad pulled them out of thin air as he studied me. "Nic, I know you care passionately about God's name—and your own. But violence is not the answer."

I sighed. I knew he was right—and that didn't solve any of my problems. "What was I supposed to do? Let him laugh at me?"

Dad shrugged. "That's what Jesus did."

I avoided his stare.

He reached out and touched my shoulder. "I know it hurts when people make fun of who you are. I deal with it every single day at work. But Jesus could let people laugh because He knew who He was; He didn't need their approval. Did you need Wesley's approval?"

When I didn't answer right away, he pinched my shoulder. "No," I begrudgingly admitted. *Some respect would have been nice, though.*

Dad kneaded my shoulder. "You're a brave kid, Nic, and passionate. I'm proud of you for not being ashamed of your faith, but throwing acid in people's faces won't win them over. You're not protecting God when you do that—you're only protecting yourself."

I sagged under his strong grip. "I'm sorry, Dad."

"Don't apologize to me. You need to apologize to Wesley."

I cringed. "But I—"

Turns out fate had a much crueler punishment planned for me, because at that moment someone screamed my dad's name. "Von!"

We both turned to see Dr. Crusher storming towards us across the lab. I panicked. Dr. Crusher was another scientist who wanted Dad's job but was too stupid to qualify.

He also happened to be Wesley's dad.

He stopped in the doorway. "What's the meaning of this, Von?"

My dad pushed me behind him. "I was just coming to find you. I've had a talk with Nic about his actions—"

"Not that." Dr. Crusher flicked his hand, like me almost burning his son's face off was a minor offense. "I meant about the Bibles."

My dad stiffened. I grabbed his arm as a frantic prayer left my consciousness.

Oh God, help.

Wesley peeked out from around his dad's lab coat, and I felt my rage returning.

Dr. Crusher savored the moment of power. "Transmitting from Mars, Von? That's a serious offense."

"What do you want, Jack?" my dad challenged, tone even.

Dr. Crusher laughed. "I'll get whatever I want after I turn you in." He gestured, and two more scientists materialized from the shadows in the lab.

Anger and fear battled for control of my nerves, and fear was winning. *Please don't do this, God! I'm sorry!*

"Paul," Dr. Crusher said with a grin, "it's my great pleasure to inform you that you're under arrest."

*

That night was the first time I ever had a nightmare.

It wasn't that I'd never had scary dreams before. Most of my dreams would terrify mere mortals. Even my mom, the only person I shared my dreams with, was disturbed by a lot of them.

My dreams never scared me, no matter how dark and devasting they were, because I only ever dreamed about what could be. My dreams weren't reality; they were *possibilities.* Some, arguably, were probabilities, the most likely solution to the math problem that was life. But no matter how realistic they were, there was no reason to be afraid of my dreams, because they could all be prevented.

Not anymore.

Suddenly, I was dreaming about things that were. That night, it was about my dad, locked in a dark cell somewhere while the government sentenced him to years upon years in prison. It was augmented, of course—there were monsters and fire and blood in places they shouldn't have been—but it was still reality.

And that's when I knew my gift had become a curse. I was dreaming of futures I couldn't change, stories I couldn't rewrite. These were dreams I couldn't control.

The next morning, they transported Dad to the nearest settlement for further questioning. There was some debate about what to do with me. Jails and foster homes were both in short supply on Mars, so after much-heated argument, it was decided that I would stay on the station under the watchful eye of another scientist until we could be deported to Earth.

My supervisor made me do school the next day like nothing had happened. It would be another week before the next transit flight, and in the meantime, the government had an education obligation to fulfill. So I was escorted to the conference room and made to sit through another series of pedantic video lectures. I turned in zeros on all my coursework that day.

Let them flunk me. I knew they wouldn't have the courage.

They refused to let me call my dad after school, so I ended up back in the lab. My access should have been revoked after the fight yesterday, but Dr. Crusher was so caught up in seizing my dad's throne that he'd forgotten to report it. So, I let myself back into the lab and resumed my acid experiments, hoping everyone on base would be smart enough to leave me alone.

I thought the challenge of actual science would distract me, but it didn't. Instead, I ended up standing at the table, holding the vial that had almost been my murder weapon in my hand, and wondering if this was all my fault.

It was my fault Dr. Crusher knew about the Bibles. I trusted Wesley, let him in on the one secret that could kill us all, and for what? A chance at a friendship that would expire as soon as our mission ended?

You're a fool.

I clenched the vial in my hand, tightly, viciously. The fragile glass shuddered in my grip, and I relished the feeling of danger. Anything was better than the rage of guilt.

And then I heard a crack, and I stopped.

My father's words whispered back to me. *You're only protecting yourself.*

I opened my hand and rubbed the hairline fracture I'd created in the glass. Maybe—maybe Dad was right. Maybe I should have been nicer to Wesley. If I hadn't threatened him, maybe he wouldn't have told his father about the Bibles. Maybe, if I had let the insult slide like my dad told me to, this never would have happened.

Or maybe... I thought as I weighed the vial in my hand, *I didn't go far enough.*

I whipped around to face the whiteboard. My unfinished equation stared back at me like a film on pause. I began running the numbers, forging the compound in my mind and imagining how the acid would burn and scar.

If only I'd had a jar of it when Dr. Crusher threatened us.

I swiped my sleeve across the board to erase the broken half of the equation and grabbed a fresh marker. My nightmare was about to get a new ending.

2062
FOURTEEN YEARS AGO

4

I hated parties.

As a general rule, they involved too many people and too little productivity. State dinners were even worse, as the majority of the attendees had no business being there. The dregs of society tended to wash up at government events, floating in on the sponsorship of privileged friends. They would cling like mollusks to affluent attendees, muddying the waters for those of us who had actual work to accomplish.

That's the only reason I came to this particular government function. I had been presented with an award and was a keynote speaker, but the only thing I wanted to walk away with was more sponsors for my experiments.

On account of said award, I could have had anyone in the room I wanted, but most of them were not worth my time. Because of the sensitive nature of my work, I needed a very specific kind of patron.

Those in the upper echelons of society weren't worth the risk; they had everything to lose and nothing to gain. Those in the lower ranks didn't have the resources I needed. But the aspiring politicians in the middle—those were my primary targets. They had enough money to be useful to me, and they had everything to gain. An underappreciated director with a shot at a higher seat was willing to bend the rules if it meant winning valuable allies. If I found one who was disgruntled enough, they might even be willing to help me break the system entirely.

I spent the evening filtering the crowd, searching for the up-and-coming. I would introduce myself, allow them to flatter themselves a bit, and then sow a seed of hope—the mere suggestion that I could be useful to them. Then I would walk away, leaving them to simmer in their imagination for a while. By the time I returned, they were ready to sign.

It was a delicate process that involved balancing a dozen active leads simultaneously. I couldn't afford to get distracted—which was why I was extremely annoyed when the daughter of Chairman Mong approached me.

Anyone else would have been beside themselves. As third in line to the General Secretary, Chairman Mong had earned the privilege of not talking to people. Instead, he spied out his prey from across the room and sent one of his lesser councilmen to make the arrangements.

His daughter, a chairwoman of some standing in her own right, also had the honor of being his carrier pigeon. She spent the evening watching his face for subtle nods and gestures. I knew this because she and I had inadvertently exchanged several glances.

As she strode towards me, her clicking stilettos heralding her approach, I realized that those glances may have been intentional on her part.

I decided to cut her off at the pass in hopes of keeping the intrusion brief. I met her halfway across the ballroom and offered my hand. "Madame Mong, I'm Dr. Nic."

She clasped my hand with a fearless grip. "Shi Min Tai," she offered.

I blinked. She'd skipped at least three phases of formal introduction and jumped straight to given names.

Well, that escalated quickly.

"Charmed," I said, and lightly pumped her hand. "Which do you prefer?"

"Excuse me?"

"If we are going on a first name basis, three given names seems excessive. Which do you prefer?"

She grinned, showing perfect teeth. "The boys in Washington call me Asia." She withdrew her hand from mine, slowly, her fingers brushing my palm. "But I prefer Min."

I hesitated, fully aware of the risks associated with that invitation.

She waited patiently.

I accepted the offer. "Pleasure to meet you, Min." In exchange, I offered her one of my rare smiles—the most valuable currency I had on me at the moment.

She seemed pleased with the sacrifice. "Congratulations on the award. From what I've heard, you deserve it."

"You seem to think so."

My prophetic insight stumped her, as it did with everyone. She arched one thin, penciled eyebrow. "I'm sorry?"

"Forgive me for noticing, but your father didn't send you over here."

She instinctively glanced back at him. Chairman Mong hadn't paid me any mind all evening, for which I was grateful. I was not interested in bargaining with him; he was one of the people I hoped would suffer when I succeeded.

No, Min had sought me out of her own volition—a fact I found extremely suspicious.

When she turned back to me, her dark eyes glinted like stars swallowed by a black hole. "You're a smart man, Nic."

"I wouldn't be worth your time if I wasn't." I shifted and glanced around the room. Several jealous—and prying—eyes were angled in our direction, no doubt wondering what wizardry I had pulled to secure Min's attention. Whatever she wanted, she'd better make it fast.

I turned back to her and spread my hands. "What can I do for you, Min?"

She devoured my subservience with a ravenous grin. "I want to sponsor your project."

"I'd be honored," I said, even though I wasn't. I did not like people who volunteered their money without first listening to my speech. That meant they had something to gain—something I hadn't sold them. "May I ask what interests you about my work?"

She opened her diamond-encrusted clutch and rifled through the contents. "The science speaks for itself, doesn't it?"

Of course it did—but not to people like Min. My project was, by design, deceptively mundane. I had developed a unique blend of plastic that was resistant to almost every acidic compound on the spectrum. The result had significant implications for the medical and industrial fields, but that was hardly the kind of advancement that concerned people of Min's status.

She withdrew a lipstick from her purse. "I think the science has other... uses, don't you?"

It did. That was the whole reason I developed it—because I ultimately intended to store something other than cleaning products in the canisters.

And that was exactly why I had to be very careful about who got involved.

I pretended to straighten my bowtie. "Is the Chairman interested in other applications?"

"Hardly." With a deft hand, she swiped a fresh layer of bloodred paint on her lips. "But I might be."

"'Might'?" I fought the urge to laugh. "As much as I love a good experiment, that is not a probability I want to test."

She clicked her lipstick case shut. "Not a man to take a risk, are we, Dr. Nic?"

The insult tickled my rage, and I realized I'd lost the upper hand in the conversation a long time ago. "I am quite comfortable taking risks," I snapped. "But only necessary ones."

"As am I. I hate an unnecessary mess." She dropped the lipstick in her purse and looked up at me. "But I can assure you this is a well-calculated risk."

Clearly, she was now trying to sell me on the deal, so I deferred the stage to her. "What are your terms?"

"I have some personal projects you may be able to help me with in the future." She looked up and met my eyes. "But in the meantime, I've looked at your portfolio. I know people who can fund everything on your list. I would be happy to introduce you."

I filtered her words through my mental translation program, trying to decode any pauses or inflections that might tell me what she was up to. If I said yes, I'd be dancing with the devil; her father could ruin me with a finger snap.

But if she meant what she said, I could have everything I wanted—and a clear shot at her father when I was ready to take it.

I held out my hand. "I expect my project to cost a great deal of money."

She took it with a smile. "Leave it to me."

✻

"I'm so glad you made it!"

I turned to see Min floating towards me across the ballroom. I accepted the hand she extended and dipped my head. "I wouldn't miss it."

I didn't tell her that I'd almost thrown the invitation away. In this digital age, messages that came in paper envelopes were rarely good news, especially when they were emblazoned with the United seal. I usually ignored paper mail as long as possible, then threw it away if I didn't like the contents. After all, the United postal service was so unreliable—it was easy for mail to get lost.

But as I'd gone to toss the envelope in the trash, I'd flipped it over and noticed her handwritten note on the back:

HOPE TO SEE YOU THERE –MIN

I'd given her the benefit of the doubt and opened the envelope, revealing an invitation to the annual United state dinner in Beijing, the most prestigious event of the year. I'd stood there, gaping at the gilded linen card, vacillating between exhilaration and abject horror.

I was exhilarated because this was my chance to become one of them—to win over some prestigious sponsors and secure my own lab so I could practice my seditious science in peace. I was horrified because Min clearly thought this was a date.

It had been a few months since we'd met, and she'd been feeding me a steady stream of middling sponsors. It was enough to keep me invested in our relationship, but not enough to make me want to commit and reveal the full details of my project.

She seemed content with the balance of power. She contacted me constantly, but she never asked about the science. She didn't demand to see reports or inquire about progress. I don't think she cared what I did with the money at all. Instead, she wanted to talk about me. She plied me mercilessly with questions about myself, my family, my interests—knowing full well that I was in no position to turn her down.

She was teasing me, but to what end, I hadn't yet figured out.

I considered refusing the invitation, but I wasn't about to sacrifice my one chance at fame and fortune. So I rallied my courage, bought a nicer bowtie, and dressed the part.

Min had also dressed for the occasion. She wore a fitted dress that flowed off her frame like water, the ruffled hem barely grazing the ground. It was black and woven with the tiniest crystals, making it look like she was clothed in starlight. Her straight black hair was pinned up with diamonds and her neck was chained in pearls.

And her lips were, as always, the color of murder.

She basked in my scrutiny. "How do I look?" she taunted, running a pale hand through her dark mane.

She was stunning, although I daren't tell her that in polite company. I stared at her, suddenly unable to find words around the buzz in my head. Every compliment I could find seemed inadequate, and I realized, far too late to back out, that she wanted more than science out of our relationship.

Her appearance sent a clear message, and unfortunately, I could read.

She spared me the misery of coming up with a gentlemanly reply. "You look handsome," she praised.

"I was just wondering if I was underdressed." I tugged on my bowtie.

She pretended to ponder that. "You could lose the mustache."

"What?" I reflectively touched it with both hands. "You don't like it, do you?"

She winked. Before I could object further, she passed a glass into my hand and gestured at me to follow her. "Come on, there's someone I'd like you to meet."

So meet and greet we did. Min led me through the crowd and introduced me to her prime contacts, forging connections like a spider weaves a web. I let her exchange the pleasantries, and then I took over, selling my captive audience with a vision of influence and prestige.

Min posed at my elbow all night. She stood far enough away to be professional, but close enough to be an accessory in my entourage. The effect was magnetic: Like a light of wealth and power, she drew the moths to me, and I caught them. By the time the evening was winding to a close, I had signed four contracts and obtained phone numbers that could lead to a dozen more.

I was more than satisfied with the night's work, but Min was still on the hunt. "I saved the best for last," she whispered as she touched my elbow and steered me towards one final victim. It was an older Asian man who I was sure I'd seen on the news at some point.

"Councilor Wu," Min called, and I abruptly remembered where I'd seen his face. Wu was the state councilor over the

North American region; he was the liaison between the entire Eastern Seaboard and the United leadership in Beijing. If I wanted my experiments shielded from government scrutiny, this was the man to talk to.

He turned to Min with a smile, face lost in welcoming wrinkles. "Miss Mong! Who have you brought me?"

He knows what's up. I bowed for respect, then offered my hand. "Dr. Nic, and it's my pleasure, sir."

He returned both gestures. "I am sure the pleasure will be all mine by the time we're done. Forgive me for asking, but I'm not familiar with your work. Is Nic your given or surname?"

I swallowed a groan. "Given, sir. My surname is not worth the breath it takes to say."

Most people accepted the joke with a chuckle and moved on. He, however, paused expectantly.

Min unwittingly cursed me by offering, "It's Von Nieuwenhuyse."

His face scrunched again, but this time, the creases were not endearing. "As in the famous Dr. Paul Von Nieuwenhuyse?"

"I like to think I'm the famous doctor now." I forced a laugh. I hated winning sponsorships based on my father's merit. Those people always ended up disappointed, because I was not my father.

The councilor, apparently, had already decided to be disappointed in me. He tipped his head and regarded me with the most vilest of expressions: pity. "It's a shame."

"Excuse me?" I snapped, even though I knew exactly what he was talking about.

"The court case. It's a shame he wouldn't accept the settlement—Mars will feel his loss."

"What's a shame is how your government is treating him," I hissed, too quickly to process that I had used real words.

Min sucked in her breath, a sharp sound through clenched teeth. The councilor was merely amused. "I take it you don't agree with their decision."

I answered that with a huff. I thought it was an inane decision. In response to my father's repeated religious infractions, they'd voted to ground him; he was no longer allowed to travel off-planet. It was a suicidal ruling on the United's part. They were denying themselves of their best colonization scientist; they'd be lucky if the whole mission didn't fail without him.

But even worse was watching my father's soul suffocate when he received the sentence. He would never get to see his precious Mars again.

At least he wouldn't until I completed my experiments.

Min seemed to recognize her error in introducing me and struggled to compensate. She laid one hand on each of our arms, as if she could forge a bridge with her presence. "Yes, it's a shame, but Nic doesn't share his father's beliefs."

I glared at her. *Have you even met me, woman?*

"Excellent," Wu slithered. "Because I can only trust my projects to men of science."

I turned back to him. "Meaning?"

He gestured vaguely, as if my religious identity was a crumb he could sweep off the table. "Well, someone who holds so fiercely to ancient mythology can't be a follower of the scientific process, now can they?"

I thought you were smart.

He watched me, eyebrow arched, waiting. It was a challenge, a test. And this was a test I was happy to fail.

I drew back and opened my mouth, but Min pinched my elbow. I started and glanced back at her. She leaned closer, her sculpted fingernails digging into my arm.

Subtly, very subtly, she shook her head.

I weighed my options. I could tell Councilor Wu what I really thought—that he was an idiot—and have the momentary satisfaction of proving that I would not be bullied.

Or I could let the offense slide and get everything I wanted. If my mission succeeded, no Christian, including my father, would ever have to suffer the United's intolerance again.

I popped my jaw and rearranged my face into my coldest smile. "Of course not, sir. Of course not."

2066
TEN YEARS AGO

5

I was so close.

I told myself that every morning, even if it wasn't true. I had to set the tone; I had to walk into work believing with every fiber of my being that today was the day. That's what my sponsors needed to see—their generosity was mathematically correlated to my level of optimism.

But some days, I needed to hear it as much as they did. I wasn't a fan of talking to myself—it took twice as long to finish a thought that way—but I indulged in it while I ruefully shaved my face each morning. I told myself I was a genius, and charismatic, and courageous. I convinced myself that I would win more sponsors, complete the project, and save the world.

At least one of those statements was hyperbole, but if I hadn't slathered myself with flattery each morning, I would have given up years ago.

It wasn't that I didn't believe in the science. The science was brilliant. What I wasn't convinced of was my own ability.

The premise was simple enough: Develop an acid that could dissolve metal, plastic, glass, and concrete alike. With such a weapon, I could melt prime military and government targets off the map. It was the kind of weapon you only needed to use once, maybe twice, and I liked that level of efficiency.

The question, of course, was *how* to weaponize it. Bomb dispersal would be dramatic for a demonstration but too localized to win a war. Using a tanker truck and firehose was the cheap but childish option.

My favorite theory was crop dusting. Disperse the liquid weapon from the air and let it rain down fire and brimstone. I'd sadistically named it Red Rain to capture the spirit.

There were some complications with that plan; if released too high, the weapon would simply evaporate. But those were problems that could be solved; dispensing the weapon was merely a matter of physics. It was the base formula that was eluding me.

It was the same problem that had frustrated me while trying to mutilate Wesley's cars all those years ago. Metal, plastic, glass, and concrete all had unique properties, which meant they were reactive to unique acidic compounds. Add in the fact that there were different *types* of metal and plastic, and I had given myself the improbable assignment of creating a compound that reacted to all of them.

Or at least most of them. I would have loved to be able to dissolve an entire city in one swipe, mainly so that I could relieve Earth of the burden of Washington and Beijing. But I would settle for crippling infrastructure. As long as there was nowhere to run and nowhere to hide, my weapon would suffice.

Unfortunately, even after years of research, I was no closer to finding a compound with the right balance. I'd discovered at least half a dozen new acidic compounds with glorious applications for the medical and industrial fields. I'd secured numerous research grants and won almost as many useless awards. But none of those formulas had any value to me. I didn't care about anything unless it would help me break the United.

Min was patient. I'd progressively revealed more and more of my research to her. She still didn't have full access to my files, but she knew enough that, if she was at least half as smart as she appeared, she could infer what was going on.

She hadn't objected. She occasionally asked for a progress report, but I think she did it more to humor me than anything else. As long as we went on our weekly dinner date every Tuesday, she was content.

I was less so. I wasn't afraid of failure; being in the experimental sciences demanded that one make friends with failure. But there was an invisible line that separated the hypothetical from the fantastical, and I was worried that I had begun to cross it.

I was neck—or, rather, arm—deep in another failed test when the secretary paged me to let me know I had a visitor. With the help of Councilor Wu, I'd been given my own lab, an entire wing at a secluded research facility. It came with state-of-the-art equipment, endless materials, and complete privacy. Absolutely nothing in the lab connected to the internet without my permission, meaning my research was shielded from government scrutiny.

But the best perk was the lady at the front desk. She afforded me the luxury of turning away visitors, a service for which I paid her in smiles and coffee delivery.

"Dr. Nic," her voice crackled sweetly over the intercom. "There's someone here to see you."

"Not today, Athena," I answered as I struggled to yank my hands out of the Teflon gloves that allowed me to manipulate the testing chamber.

Normally she obeyed me the first time, but today she was feeling impertinent. "It's your father."

I groaned. Normally I let my father up without question, but that would not be wise today. I knew what he wanted to talk about, and it was too soon. He needed at least three more days to cool off.

"Today's a bad day," I answered.

There was a painful pause. "He agrees, sir. He says it's a very sorry day indeed."

I yanked my goggles off and threw them on the table. "Send him up."

I quickly flicked off the computer monitor, tucked the most telling papers under a folder, and pulled the projector screen over the whiteboard. My dad didn't know what I was working on, and today was definitely not the day to have that conversation.

The automatic door whooshed open. He stood there, arms crossed, feet apart, nostrils flared—and said absolutely nothing.

"If you don't step inside, that door is going to close again," I informed him.

He did so. His graying hair was unwashed and his mustache was running rampant across his upper lip. In the harsh light of the lab, the dark circles under his eyes made it look like he'd been punched in the face. He probably hadn't slept since he'd gotten the news.

When he still refused to initiate the conversation, I decided to be the better man. "I would give you an explanation of why I did it, but I don't think you're in a frame of mind to hear it yet."

"I don't need an explanation," he snapped. "I know exactly what you did and why you did it. You think I can't take care of my own daughter."

"Who is my sister," I reminded him, "if the structure of our family tree was in question."

"Well, you seem to have forgotten that I am also your father. Nic, what's gotten into you? Do you know how upset your mother is?"

"Yes, I know, she's tried to call me ten times." I didn't add how much it had killed me to ignore each of her calls. But I knew my mother, and I knew that we spoke the same language. When we're upset, we lose our filters, and we burn bridges like matchsticks. I didn't want my relationship with my mother to be tainted by all the things she—we—would say in the heat of the moment, so I'd silenced her calls.

"Then you must understand what this is doing to her. What were you thinking, calling CPS?"

"I was thinking about Cea," I returned. "Which is what you should have done."

If my father had been more like me, I would have expected a violent reaction to that statement. Instead, he struggled to properly express his frustration and ended up flinging his arms around like a strangled turkey. "You really think I don't care about my own children? Who do you take me for?"

I leaned my knuckles on the workstation. "Do you want an honest answer to that?"

He hesitated, then folded his arms across his chest. "Yes. I do."

I took a deep breath and ordered my words—like I would when I was trying to convince a sponsor that this was for his own good. "I think you're a brilliant man and an amazing father. But you're picking fights with hornets—fights you can't win—and you're putting Cea in danger."

My words gave him pause, but not long enough of one. "Nic, all we did was go to church—like you used to do."

I ignored the cheap shot. "That, and you tried to transmit illegal media from work even though the conditions of your parole clearly state the consequences for such an act."

Any camaraderie I had generated by complimenting his parenting skills washed away. "They're called Bibles," he corrected. "And since when have I been concerned with the consequences? Since when have *you* been concerned with the consequences?"

In his defense, he had a point. I didn't care about consequences, but I did care about winning. And when you're playing the long game, sometimes you have to lose some battles to win the war.

As soon as Red Rain was complete, I would kick the hornet's nest. But until then, I would avoid aggravating the hive. My father, on the other hand, seemed determined to get stung.

I didn't expect him to agree with my philosophy, but he still deserved an honest response. "In case you didn't read the court order, those 'consequences' involved a federal raid of your home, your access to public accommodations being restricted, and a sleepover at the prison—your third in so many months, I might add."

"I'll move into the prison before I let them take the Bible *or* my daughter from me," he snarled.

I rolled my eyes, and apparently that was going a step too far. He burned as red as Mars as he took a dramatic step towards me. "Nic Joseph Von Nie—"

"I'm listening," I cut him off.

"No, you're not, and that's the problem." Abruptly, he seemed to reach the astute conclusion that I wasn't going to grovel before his anger. He sighed, and his whole body sagged, as if rage was the only thing holding his muscles taut. "Nic, please. You need to talk to them. Recant your statement. Don't take Cea away."

"She's not being 'taken away,' Dad." I tried to soften my tone, vainly hoping that would invite him to see reality. "She's just at boarding school. She's literally twenty-two minutes and fifteen seconds from home. You can visit her."

"Yes, on Wednesdays and Saturdays," he snapped with absolutely no gratitude at all, "like she's in prison."

"It's better than her *actually* being in prison." I grunted and rearranged the vials in the holder on the table in front of me. I probably shouldn't handle caustic chemicals right now, but if I didn't busy my hands, they'd find something far more unhelpful to do.

My dad didn't respond, maybe, for once, because he agreed with me.

"Dad, I know you think I'm on their side, but I promise I'm just doing it to protect Cea." I tapped the glass containers and tried to steady my thoughts. "Every time you go to jail, she spends the night in some state house for girls, and one day, they're not going to let her come home. I don't want to see her end up with strangers—or in prison with you."

My dad was still silent, so I chanced a glance up at him.

I regretted my decision when I saw his eyes were blurred with tears. "So you sent her to an indoctrination camp full of people who hate her religion? Nic, have you even been there?"

"Yes, I toured the place before I recommended it." Despite the mediocre curriculum, it was better than prison.

He shook his head, but the motion was wobbly, imbalanced. "Nic, you don't understand. Please, don't do this to her—let alone your mother. I can't lose my daughter. Not after I've already lost my son."

I rubbed my temples. "You haven't 'lost' me, Dad. I'm literally home for dinner twice a week."

He tipped his head back, his gaze long and deep, like I was a chemical equation to be solved. "Haven't I?"

I looked away. "It's not forever." I spoke of Cea, but the statement applied to both of us.

"So when?" my father challenged. He finally came around the table to stand beside me. "When are my children coming home? What are you waiting for?"

I'm waiting until I'm powerful enough to keep the monster from assimilating us back in.

"What are you working on, Nic?"

His tone shifted, downwards, and I knew I had to end the conversation quickly. "I told you, Dad. I have a research grant from the medical board—"

"Nic, I'm not stupid, and neither are you. I know you're not just creating solvents for the hospital. You're planning something."

"I'm always planning something," I deadpanned. "Now I need to get back to work." I grabbed his elbow and herded him towards the door. He allowed me to steer him around the table—and then his eyes fell on the testing chamber, where a warped puddle of plastic represented my latest roadblock.

He studied it, his eyes blinking like a cursor tracking across a monitor. And then, like clouds blowing across the moon, sadness cloaked his expression.

He'd seen this all before.

I tugged on his arm. "Let's go, Dad."

He looked up at me. "You're creating a weapon, aren't you?"

"Dad, I told you, I have a grant—"

"Don't lie to me!" he shouted. His voice nearly cracked from the sheer weight of the pain it carried. He twisted his arm from my grasp and whipped around to face the whiteboard. Before I could stop him, he yanked on the cord and rolled the projector screen up with a snap, revealing the formula for Red Rain.

The equation wasn't complete, but someone with his intelligence could easily decode what I was attempting. He read the sequence once, twice, three times, his face twisting in recognition.

"Son," he breathed, the word choking at the top of his throat. "What have you done?"

"I haven't *done* anything yet. The formula's incomplete."

He shook his head. "Not for long," he said, his grief muddying the compliment that was so strongly implied.

I took a long, even breath, forcing my nerves back under my control. "Dad, this is none of your business. Please leave."

"None of my business?" Horror washed his aging face white. "Son, do you understand what this weapon would do?"

"Why do you think I'm creating it?" I hissed.

"Are you trying to start another world war? Because that's what this does." He flung both hands at the whiteboard, as if I wasn't fully aware of what I was creating.

"I'm not trying to start a war, I'm trying to win one."

"By burning people to death with acid?"

A lifetime of doubt, distrust, and utter disappointment was crammed into those ten syllables. I could have argued with him; I had a whole thirty-page report proving that the collateral damage would be minimal if we bombed a few key targets. I had no intention of committing genocide.

But explaining that to my father would have been a waste of breath.

"Son, you have to stop this." It wasn't a suggestion. "Delete the data. Now."

I folded my arms. "I've made up my mind, Dad. People are counting on me."

"Nic, no, please. You don't understand. I can't let you do this." He had the audacity to reach out and grab my shoulder.

I shrugged him off. "I'm not asking you to be a part of it."

"Son, listen to me!" His voice broke and bent, as if modulating the pitch could shatter the glass between us. "This isn't you. I know it isn't. I know you're a kind, caring—"

"Stop," I said, more to myself than to him. I took a generous step back from him and closed my eyes, searching for my center that had been mercilessly kicked to a dusty corner of my mind. I waited until my emotions had settled before speaking again. "We don't have to do this."

He searched me. "I do."

"No, you don't. Dad, I'm an adult. We don't have to agree. You don't have to understand me." I spoke the words with false conviction.

The anger evaporated from his face, leaving a watery grief that made me feel like I was already dead and buried. "You're right, son. I don't have to agree with you. But I do have to protect you—even from yourself."

I turned back to the whiteboard. "Just walk away, Dad."

He did. After a moment's hesitation, he turned and walked out the door without another word.

Two days later, the police showed up at the door. They cuffed me and forced me to watch as they razed the lab and destroyed my research. Papers shredded, hard drives bashed in, all my chemical compounds poured down the drain. Eight years of work, erased in twenty minutes.

They claimed they had been tipped off by an anonymous source. But I knew who had sent them.

6

Min came to visit me in jail three days later.

I heard her heels clacking on the concrete and knew it was her long before she rounded the corner. "Nic, baby, are you okay?" she cried.

I was too surprised to answer her at first. I hadn't expected to see her or any of my sponsors ever again.

She grasped the bars of my cell and pressed her face against them, looking even more pathetic than I felt. "Are you all right? Are you hurt?"

I stood and walked over. "I'm fine. It's a county jail, not a torture bay."

Her coy smile returned, bringing the glint back into her eyes. She flicked her sharp fingers at the guard who stood behind her. "What are you waiting for? Open it up. We're going to be late, and this man needs to shave."

The guard obeyed, swiping a keycard on the door of my cell, but he didn't look pleased about the whole ordeal.

I took the implied invitation and cautiously stepped out into the hall. "Late for what? And what's going on?"

She laughed and threw her arms around me. "You're being released, you silly goose. And did you forget it's Tuesday?"

I struggled to process three stimuli at once: I was being released, she was hugging me, and I had, in fact, forgotten that it was Tuesday.

At least one of those things was completely unacceptable.

I gingerly disentangled myself from her arms. "It might be the dank prison air impairing my brain function, but I don't understand."

"What's there to understand?" She winked. "I'm a Mong."

The guard grunted something foul.

Min graciously ignored him and started waltzing down the hall, gesturing at me to follow. "Come on, my driver's waiting. You only have an hour to get cleaned up. Do you still have the reservations?"

I hurried to catch up. "Unless the government called the restaurant to tell them I was indisposed, I would assume we're still on for 6 o'clock."

"Excellent," she chirped, punctuating with a finger wave over her shoulder. "Because I have a surprise for you."

＊

"What about Mars?"

It was several hours later, and we were closing our evening with coffee and a shared dessert. In the interest of time, Min's driver had forgone my house and taken me to hers, where a butler magically produced a clean outfit in my size. Within thirty minutes I had washed the stench of incarceration from my person, and we made it to the restaurant just in time.

Min had deferred my multitude of attempts to thank her for the bailout. "It really is no trouble," she crooned, and I believed her.

She'd filled the evening with her usual routine of pleasantries and social interrogations. I was dying—and somewhat terrified—to ask her what my "surprise" was, but I knew she would not allow the dinner experience to be rushed.

Finally, she drew her tablet from her oversized designer purse and laid it on the table between us. On the screen was displayed the blueprint for a research base.

"It's yours," she declared.

I looked up at her. "You're going to have to forgive me for my relative unintelligence tonight, but I really don't follow."

She grinned. "You need to continue the project." It wasn't a request. "And you need a private place to do so."

I agreed with both of those statements. "And it's on Mars?" I wasn't sure what I found more shocking: the fact that she'd casually acquired a base on Mars in less than 72 hours, or the fact that I might get to govern it.

She shrugged. "It seemed more... secure."

I picked up the tablet and studied the schematic. "It will pose some environmental challenges for testing..."

"I would offer you a blank check, except nobody uses checks anymore." She folded her arms on the table, smirked, and waited for me to catch up.

I bought myself time by zooming in on the schematic. I couldn't argue with anything she was saying, but I was still missing one crucial piece: why she cared.

Anyone else would have ditched me at the first sign of trouble. That's what Dad's sponsors had done to him, time and again. Even I had lost a few by saying too much too soon and in the wrong company.

I realized Min had the resources to make everything go away, but it was still *work*. It took effort to pay off judges, wipe court records, and distract the media. Covering my arrest was a mess, and I knew how Min felt about those.

I looked up and searched the galaxies lost in her eyes. "And what do you get out of it? Because if I go to Mars, we'll have to reduce our dates to once every six months—and I heard the restaurants on Mars are not that great."

"They're not," she agreed. "But it's not forever, is it?"

That was the exact same thing I had said to my dad, and in that moment, I realized that Min knew exactly what was going on.

She knew I was trying to set the world on fire, and she was eager to watch it burn.

I took a slow sip of my drink. "I take it you don't have a great relationship with your father." As a top United official, he'd be one of the first to fall if I succeeded.

She stroked the stem of her glass with her fingernail. "He was never home. So..." She tipped her head to the side, her flat-ironed hair falling across her soft cheekbones. "What do you say, Dr. Nic?"

I arched an eyebrow and gave her one of the smiles she so desperately coveted. "I don't suppose I have a choice, do I?"

She laughed. "No, you don't."

✱

It was Base #9.

Well, Base #9.6.11 was the technical title, based on the entirely arbitrary coordinates system the early colonizers had conjured up. Dad claimed the system was idiotic, and I was inclined to agree, if only because Region #1 was not correlated to a static reference point like a pole or the equator. It was merely the crater where the first manned mission had landed. In any case, #9 was currently the only base in the region, so the extra numbers were superfluous.

It was a fairly old base by Martian standards, old enough that it was feasible my dad had helped lay the foundation. I couldn't decide how that fact made me feel, so I made the conscious decision not to devote any more processing power to it.

What *did* bother me was the design. The base sprawled across the valley like a toddler had spilled a bucket of blocks. Dozens of research domes were connected to a central wing by long hallways that snaked through the dirt like worms. Some wings fed into other wings, and some hallways ended in nothing at all. It was deplorably inefficient and a grotesque waste of space.

But at least there was room to grow. There was nothing but red wilderness for miles, and the nearest settlement was almost three hours away. That's just where I liked my neighbors: in a different time zone.

It was past nightfall by the time I arrived, but they'd left the lights on for me. The exterior beacons were all lit, and the docking bay doors were open to receive me. As soon as the gate sealed shut and the atmosphere was restored, the door to the lobby opened.

A wrinkled waif of a man stood there. He was of average height and build, but he was so pale, with his white lab coat and even whiter hair, that he probably would have reflected light like the moon. It looked like God had gotten careless and bleached the entire man in the washer.

"Dr. Von Nieuwenhuyse, I presume?" he said by way of greeting, and offered his hand.

I dropped my suitcase on the ground to accept the gesture and was pleased to find that he had a strong grip, which was impressive since I could feel every bone in his hand. "Just Dr. Nic," I corrected. "Or Nic if time is of the essence."

"Isn't it always?" He let go of my hand to gesture at himself. "Carnegie." He didn't add any qualifiers, which was just as well; Carnegie was already such an ostentatious name that I couldn't imagine adding any more syllables to it.

"What's your function here?" I asked as I bent to grab my suitcase off the floor.

He beat me to it, employing a frightening amount of agility. "Governor's assistant," he announced.

I hesitated, my hand posed awkwardly midair. "Then I suppose you're out of a job."

"Not unless you've brought your own people." He glanced behind me, as if verifying that I had, in fact, not brought his replacement.

I studied him. An assistant was something I desperately needed—but only if I could trust him to be more loyal to me than to the United.

He seemed to deduce the source of my hesitation. "Besides, Miss Mong said I had to play nice, or she'll remind the officials of my past, ah… indiscretions."

That was what I needed to hear. "All right then, your interview starts now. Walk and talk. I want the tour."

"As you wish." He turned, my suitcase in hand, and started walking down the main hall.

I regretted my request for a tour about five minutes in. If the outside of the base looked chaotic, the inside was even more so. The central hallway and Wings 1-12 were sensible enough, probably because they were original. After that, the layout devolved into utter nonsense. It was clear that previous governors had tacked on new wings whenever a project demanded it. The result was that rooms serving similar functions—like greenhouses—were spread out all across the base, and the numbering system was so arbitrary that they might as well have not labeled any of the doors.

As a prime example, about twenty minutes into the tour, we found ourselves in Wing 74, even though the previous hallway had contained doors labeled in the 30s.

To add insult to injury, Wing 74 wasn't even finished. I don't think it had ever been used at all. Wires and insulation sagged from the exposed ceiling, and Carnegie had to drag most of the doors open by hand.

"You're paying to oxygenate rooms that no one is using—it's a massive waste of resources." I dragged my finger across a ledge and came up with a wad of dust.

Carnegie shrugged as he opened the door at the end of the hall. "It's not my money."

I stepped through the doorway after him. "What was this room even supposed to be?" It was a stunning but useless design. The room was massive and round with a domed ceiling that arched three stories overhead. Just keeping the cavernous space at a minimal 60 degrees was probably costing the base thousands a month.

Carnegie furrowed his brow. "I'm actually not sure. Theater, perhaps?"

"Who has time for that?" I said, twisting around. But even as my eyes toured the room, a new idea started forming.

"Certainly not you." Carnegie rested his hands in the pockets of his lab coat. "What do you think, doctor? Do you find the amenities sufficient?"

"If I don't, then I'll just build something new, like everyone else has apparently done."

He acknowledged that with a chuckle. "Shall we begin at 0900 tomorrow?"

"Better make it 1000—it'll take me an hour just to walk to the lab." I stopped in the middle of the room and looked up at the ceiling—remembering, suddenly, a building on Earth with a room of this size.

A warm, soggy feeling tried to worm its way into my stomach, although whether it was hope or longing or something equally detestable, I couldn't tell. I usually didn't have time for either of those emotions, but maybe now was the time to indulge.

I finally had everything I needed. I had unlimited funds and a powerful benefactor willing to ignore laws to get me what I needed. I was completely cut off from United control; even if they did try to bust me, it would take them a week just to fly up here, and I'd see them coming from miles away. I even had a willing assistant so I wouldn't have to waste time on paltry tasks like paperwork and emails.

I could do this. I could still finish Red Rain.

I turned back to Carnegie. "We meet in the morning for a preliminary briefing. And in the meantime, I have something I want you to research. I think I have an idea for this room."

2067
NINE YEARS AGO

7

"You can't do this to me!"

That was incorrect. I was her legal guardian now, and she was still a minor, which meant I could, in fact, tell her what to do.

She knew that, of course, which was why she was resorting to hysterics. Her frazzled curls stood on end as she stomped about my office, waving her arms. She was like a little frilled lizard—doing everything she could to make herself appear bigger and more threatening.

"You can't kidnap me like this!"

I rolled my eyes, hoping that was a gesture her teenage brain could translate. "You're not a prisoner, Cea. You can go anywhere on base, and you have unrestricted internet access. You can even go off-base if you want—as long as I know where you are at all times."

Even I realized how that sounded, although regrettably, I didn't recognize it until after the words had left my mouth.

She growled like a disgruntled kitten. "You're not the boss of me! I can't believe you. You tricked me!"

That was the first accurate thing she'd said all night. I had pulled what could arguably be called a "bait and switch." I'd invited my sister to visit me at the base on Mars for the summer, and she'd excitedly accepted. It was only after she'd been here a week that I told her the truth: I had been granted full custody of her, and she wasn't going home.

Lesser men might have called me a coward, and the insult wouldn't have been inaccurate. But I knew my sister, and I knew that if I told her in advance, she never would have gotten on the transit. Not to speak of the stunts our parents might have pulled to try and keep her on Earth. No, I knew that if we'd had this conversation in advance, the police would have gotten involved, and she'd be even more shaken than she already was.

I'd gladly accept the title of coward if it meant my sister had been spared some misery.

She seemed to finally recognize that I wasn't threatened by her dramatic hand gestures, so she crossed her arms. "You can't do this to me," she said again, as if I'd find the repetition intimidating. "You're not my dad."

I gagged on the thought. "Heaven forbid," I muttered, even though that was the most ironic expression I could have chosen. "I'm not trying to parent you, Cea. I'm not about to impose an 11 pm bedtime or tell you that you can't date. All I'm trying to do is keep you alive and out of jail."

She huffed. "I don't need your help with that."

No, but our parents do, I thought, and wisely didn't say.

She resumed her war dance, strutting back and forth across the rug. "I can't believe the government just handed me over!"

It was my turn to huff. That was the most believable part of this Shakespearean tragedy, and her naivety was a little concerning. The government had been *delighted* to give me custody of my sister, so much so that they'd pushed the paperwork through in a month—an Olympic record for them. After all, I was an assimilated citizen, a prestigious governor in good standing with the officials. My parents were none of those things. They were religious noncompliants who had been in jail three times in the past two months.

That's what pushed me over the edge. I'd been contemplating requesting custody of Cea for years but had lacked the means. Now I owned a base, which gave me a stable source of income and Cea a steady place to live. I'd applied to become a foster guardian with the United, secretly hoping I would never have to use the privilege.

And then Sardis called to let me know my parents had been put in jail again. This wasn't particularly concerning in its own right, and I almost hung up on him—he had called during an important meeting, after all. But then he started describing the prison, and I knew the tides had changed.

I'd grilled him for details and quickly figured out that the place they had been sent wasn't a typical jail. No, this was something new, something that hadn't made it to the media yet. The United was getting creative with solving their unassimilated problem, and it was only a matter of time before Cea ended up behind bars with them. I immediately filed for custody and invited Cea to take a leave from boarding school and come visit me.

My parents' incarceration didn't last long. Dad pulled his usual stunts and blew the place up (somewhat literally, I was told), generating a wave of nasty media attention. To save face, the government sent them home with the usual slap on the wrist of fines and felonies. Thankfully, by the time they had been released, Cea was already on the transit to Mars.

Everyone was none the wiser until today. An officer had served the papers to my parents this morning, and I had undertaken the harrowing task of informing Cea of her new situation.

It had gone about as well as I expected.

"I'm not staying. You can't make me," she challenged, punctuating with another stomp.

"In case you've forgotten, you're only fourteen," I returned. "So as much as I'd rather find more productive things to do with my time, if I have to make you, I will."

She blistered bright red. "You're lying."

I breathed a private sigh of relief. As much as I didn't enjoy having my integrity questioned by a teenager, I knew I was about to win the argument. Cea always resorted to crucifying my character when she ran out of other options.

I reached back and grabbed my mug off the desk. "Would you like to see the court order?"

She hissed like a pot about to boil over. "Dad won't stand for this. He'll come and get me."

"I'm well aware," I grunted, taking a rallying drag of coffee, "which is why I took out a restraining order on him."

She washed white and froze, all the resistance evaporating from her body.

I stared into the mug, measuring my words. "Neither he nor Mom are supposed to contact you for six months, until they—all of you—calm down."

"How—how could you?" she whispered, the accusation rasping against her throat. "How could you do that to them? They're our *parents!*"

As if the process had given me any joy. Nothing about this abysmal situation gave me any pleasure, despite what my dad might say. But I knew the nuance of my motivations would be lost on Cea, so I didn't offer them up to be scrutinized. "I did what had to be done. You live here now, and that's final."

"No, I don't. I'm going home." She meant it as a threat, but her tears warped her voice, turning the exclamation into a pitiful cry for help.

I turned away so she couldn't see the emotion that tainted my face. "You can't. If you try to board a transit, they'll pick you up and send you right back here."

An ugly sob ripped out of her.

I pinched my eyes shut. "This is your home now, Cea," I said, forcing each syllable to be even. "The sooner you get used to it, the sooner you'll feel better."

She was unnervingly silent. I made the mistake of looking back at her.

Her swollen eyes glowed with blood and water as she glared at me. "I hate you," she hissed.

"I know," I said, my tone not belying the pain in my chest. "It was a sacrifice I was willing to make."

She shattered. She slapped her hands over her face as fresh sobs poured out of her. I could only watch her retreating form as she turned and ran out of the room.

8

I knew it was a mistake to visit my parents.

It had been about three months since I'd taken custody of Cea, and at Min's behest, I had taken a last-minute flight to Earth to attend a symposium on Martian climate change or some equally pointless topic. I should have refused; leaving Cea alone on base while she was still sulking was an unwarranted risk. Carnegie was many things, but he was not a babysitter.

But for reasons I was unwilling to admit, Min often inspired me to act against my better judgment. To her credit, I'd secured three new commissions for the base out of the event, but I knew the invitation had been a farce to get me to come visit. I'd taken the hint and booked a late dinner for tonight. What was terrifying was how much I was looking forward to it.

I had a few idle hours before I needed to pick her up, which unfortunately meant I had the perfect opportunity to visit my parents. I'd spent the entire morning trying to come up with an excuse to avoid them but couldn't find one that would withstand the test of my advanced logic. So after wasting many choice swear words on the hotel bathroom mirror, I found myself driving to Alliston.

It wasn't that I didn't want to see them. This fact seemed too nuanced for them to appreciate, but I always wanted to *see* my parents. What I didn't want to do was talk.

But I knew that, no matter what the restraining order said, there would be words. As I approached the house, I told myself that it would be better for them to crucify me than Cea. Perhaps, if I let them vent now, the next time they had a visitation with Cea they could focus on dispensing the loving attention she so desperately craved.

In some bizarre act of defiance, their porch light was on. I decided to be gracious and ring the bell instead of letting myself in the back with my key. Technically, there was nothing in the court order about me, but I was no fool. I wasn't about to walk into a den of bears robbed of their cub without knocking first.

Mom answered before the dorky electronic ring had finished playing. She opened the interior door but made no move to touch the storm door and invite me in. She stood there, staring at me from the other side of the glass, for a solid ten seconds.

I let her.

"He's here," she announced finally.

"Coming," my dad called from somewhere in the house.

"Was there traffic?" Mom asked.

I frowned. "What?"

"Took you long enough to get here," she stated blandly. "Your symposium has been over for two hours. Was there traffic?"

I allowed some emotion to make it onto my face. "You knew I was coming?"

Her nose twitched. "You're not the only one who knows how to hack into a personnel file."

I acknowledged that with a nod, even as I wondered how long she had been watching me.

Dad appeared, shrugging on a jacket. "All right, let's go. You, car." He pointed at me.

"Excuse me?"

He gave Mom a quick peck and then joined me on the porch. "Car. Let's go. We'll be late."

"Late for what?" I demanded, even though that was the least of my concerns. Visiting my parents in a house with multiple exits was one thing. Being confined in a car was an entirely different matter.

He was already walking to the detached garage. "You know they close early on Mondays. Come on, we only have an hour."

If I had thought hard enough, I probably could have remembered what closed early on Mondays, but that information was a waste of processing power when I had no intention of going. I glanced back at Mom.

Her arms had returned to their default position—tightly crossed on her chest. "You owe him this much."

I grunted and followed Dad to the car.

I had hoped mutual distrust would keep my father from attempting conversation, but I was wrong. He kept asking questions—the same ones he asked me every time he called.

How's work?

What's the latest project?

How's Sardis? He found a wife yet?

What about the base? How is it holding up? Have you upgraded the air purifier yet?

I answered the first few interrogations with clipped responses, because I falsely assumed he didn't care. After about five minutes of being brushed off, however, he slammed on the brakes at a yellow light and turned to glare at me.

"Was the restraining order against me or you?"

"What?"

"Unless I misread the paper, there was nothing in the court order that prevented us from talking about work." He turned back to the road. "So you're under no legal obligation to be rude about it."

I relaxed back in the seat. "My apologies, I thought you didn't care."

He huffed. "It's my base. I built it. Of course I care."

His words prodded the question that I was still, after all this time, too afraid to ask.

Then why don't you care about what happens to me or Cea?

He was right about one thing, though—I was under no legal or moral obligation to be rude, so I gave him what he wanted. We talked amicably about work, about all the new research projects and scientific improvements that were going on at the base, as we drove to the outskirts of the city.

When I saw the bronzed dome peaking the horizon, I abruptly remembered what closed early on Mondays.

The observatory.

"Why are we here?" I asked as we parked. They'd taken away his designated spot to save face, but they conveniently hadn't reassigned it to anyone else, so he parked in it anyway.

He didn't look back at me as we entered the building. "It seemed like a better place to talk."

"Not if you want privacy," I muttered, glancing around at the scattered visitors in the lobby.

He shrugged. "You always seemed more comfortable here than at home."

He walked up to the faculty door and pressed his thumb to the keypad. The screen squawked in warning and flashed red.

I cringed. The clerk in the ticket booth started out of her stupor and glared up at us. She looked prepared to mouth off— and then she recognized who it was.

She got out of her chair and glanced around the lobby. Satisfied that the few remaining visitors had better things to do than pay attention to us, she pressed a button to unlock the door and waved us through. Dad winked at her as he opened the door.

I followed him up to the observation dome on the top floor. Again, a half-hearted attempt had been made to strip the building of his legacy. The metal letters above the door now just read OBSERVATORY, but you could still see the ghost of his name in the faded paint.

We stepped in, and Dad toggled the controls to open the dome. I took a visual diagnostic of the room and noticed that the technology had been upgraded since I was here last. The telescope had been augmented with several new robotic instruments, and the control panel was twice as wide. I wondered who had been pouring money into the place; Dad had been fined out of most of his.

He walked over to the control panel and flicked the monitors on. "Show me the base."

"You haven't seen it?" I had a hard time believing my dad hadn't looked the base up before now. I'd been governor for over a year, and it wasn't like he didn't know where it was. It was one of his models, after all.

"I want to see how big it's gotten." He stood back to give me room at the controls.

I did not take the bait. "If you want to see the new additions, there's livecams on the promotional website that are much better."

He frowned at me. "You know, you'd save yourself a lot of energy if you didn't insist on being such a jerk all the time."

"It's how I stay fit." I sighed and rubbed my forehead. "What's this really about, Dad? I know you didn't drag me out here just to stargaze."

"Maybe I did." He keyed coordinates into the screen. The whole room vibrated as the telescope began roaming automatically, searching the skies for an unseen target. "Not everything I do is rocket science. Maybe I'm just an old man wanting to look up at the stars with his son one last time."

I didn't want to believe that. I would have rather dealt with rocket science.

The telescope stopped. The viewscreen flickered on, and a crystal-clear image of Mars filled the life-size monitor. Dad tipped his head back and studied it.

"Maybe... maybe I just want to know where my children are."

The silence returned, hot and heavy.

I walked over to the control panel. I stretched my fingers over the keyboard, then stopped.

I unplugged the handheld touchpad from the panel and passed it to my dad. "You drive. I'll show you."

His face stretched in a small smile as he took the device from me.

I gave Dad directions as he navigated the telescope across the surface of the planet. Thankfully it was the right time of day, and the base, which sat just north of the equator, was in full view. Whoever had invested in the telescope had not wasted their money; the image was stunning, and we could zoom in so close that you could almost see the spider legs of the base stretching out into the valley.

"Do you like living there?" Dad asked after we'd appreciated the view in silence for a minute.

My personal preferences had not been a factor in choosing the base, but I daren't tell him the real reason I was up there. I shrugged. "Better than Earth."

"That's setting the bar real low, isn't it?" He chuckled, but the sound died before it was finished. "And what about Cea? Does she like it?"

I stiffened. "I don't think she's decided yet."

Dad's lips twitched. "If she's anything like you, she'll take to it like a fish to water."

Cea wasn't anything like me, but I was inclined to agree. She would learn to appreciate life on base, once she realized I was giving her privacy from the government's merciless scrutiny.

If only my dad could recognize what I was doing for my family.

I decided to rip the bandage off. "Are you mad I took custody of Cea?"

He shook his head. "They were going to take her anyway."

"What?" I exclaimed. I wasn't surprised that the government had been planning to put Cea in the system; what shocked me was that Dad seemed so resigned to it.

He nodded, his eyes wandering across the dome. "It was only a matter of time. I think the only reason they hadn't done it yet was they knew I'd raise a storm in the media, and they needed a good story to cover it."

I knew that was the truth. That's why I'd gotten a restraining order—to try and save my family a little dignity.

"No, what bothers me is that I don't think she's any safer with you than she is with them."

I jerked my head up to find his eyes boring into mine, cold and unforgiving.

"I'm sorry?" I spat. I didn't usually waste energy on being offended, but now seemed like an excellent occasion. "You'd rather she be in the hands of a psychotic government than with her own *brother*?"

He folded his arms across his chest. "I wish you would have left her in that boarding school."

"Oh, you mean 'indoctrination camp full of people who hate her religion'?" I threw his own words back at him.

He was prepared for the volley. "Last I checked, so do you."

I pinched the bridge of my nose. "I don't know what that word means to you, but I don't 'hate' your religion."

"It used to be your religion, too."

In his defense, I walked right into that one, but I was prepared to walk right back out. I put my hands up. "I'm not having this conversation with you."

"Then don't."

I arched an eyebrow. He shrugged. "You can leave. No one's making you stand here and talk to your old man. You're the one that came to visit me."

"A gesture that was apparently wasted." I glanced at the door and contemplated taking his suggestion.

"Then why'd you come?"

I turned around. He spread his hands. "Why'd you come? You know my opinions haven't changed."

"I'm well aware," I admitted. "But if you're going to insist on preaching this sermon, I'd rather you do it to me than Cea."

"If you think a restraining order is going to stop me from parenting my own child, then those PhDs are wasted on you. I will never stop trying to train my daughter." He sighed, and some of the sting left his voice. "Just like I'll never give up on my son."

Against all better judgment, I looked up and met his eyes.

"I know what you're doing, Nic," he said, voice glimmering with sadness. "I know what you're building on that base."

"Dad," I hissed, and hoped the room wasn't recorded.

He spread his hands. "Don't worry, you won't get any trouble from me. I learned my lesson—I know I can't stop you. I just wonder if there's room for me and your mother up there."

A shot of hope stabbed me, and I foolishly grabbed it. Was my dad asking to come to Mars? "All you have to do is say the word, Dad, and I can have you on the next transit. I know the people."

He shook his head. "That's not what I meant. I meant, is there room for me in your perfectly balanced ideology?"

"I don't know what you think my 'ideology' is..." I swallowed the sarcasm and braced myself, fully aware of the risk I was taking with my next words. "But there's always room for you in my life."

He smiled, and for one final moment, the world was right on its axis.

"I love you too, son." He blinked and failed to stop the tears from forming. "But you know that's not true."

The tectonic plates shifted, and I felt the magma of rejection seeping in. "So I'm a liar now?"

He didn't deny it. "Let's say I come with you. Am I allowed to disagree with how you run things?"

"I feel obliged to tell you that this is a completely ineffective use of the rhetorical question," I snapped, "but yes. I'm not afraid of your opinions."

As soon as the words left my mouth, I realized with a pinch in my chest how untrue they were—although not for the reasons he would have assumed.

"Neither is the government." He shrugged. "I can have an opinion. I just can't act on it."

"I'm pleased to inform you that there will be plenty of room in my… on my base for people to experiment with whatever they wish. Which you would know if you'd listen to me."

My statement must not have been as accusing as it sounded in my head, because he didn't flinch. "Perhaps, until it interferes with one of your experiments. What happens if I don't like what you're doing? What if I try to stop it? What are you going to do—lock me in my room?"

I groaned. "I'm thinking about it."

He shook his head. "No, Nic, you and I both know that there's only room in your universe for people who agree with you. As soon as someone threatens your power, you won't hesitate to toss them aside to protect yourself. Then you'll be no better than the United is—willing to kill anything or anyone who threatens your control."

I should have been angry. Anger would have been the safer way to end this conversation. But instead, I was a fool and chose grief.

"Is that what you think of me?" I whispered, my voice barely loud enough to breach the chasm between us. "I'm not a killer."

He didn't even hesitate. "You will be if you complete your experiment."

That wasn't true. I had dozens of reports, statistics, and simulations demonstrating how my weapon would save lives. I could prove it mathematically—and morally.

But I didn't try. I didn't want to. I just closed my eyes and tried to rearrange my reality around the fact that formed the black hole at the center of my universe: My dad would never understand.

"Nic—son." His voice shifted through a roulette of emotions as if he were trying to find the tone that would save our relationship. "You're a kind, caring young man."

"You don't really believe that," I muttered, and tried to make myself believe it. If only I could bend time and space and convince twelve-year-old me that his father didn't mean what he said. That all those words spoken over him were lies, and he would never measure up.

Maybe then I wouldn't have wasted so many years trying.

"And you're brilliant. You're gifted, Nic—and I don't mean with a science degree. I know you can see things, comprehend a reality others can't. I've known since you were born that you were destined to change the world. That's how you got this far— you wouldn't be doing what you're doing if you didn't think the world could be saved."

In a cruel irony, that was the most validating thing my father had ever said to me.

Then why won't you help me save it?

"But we both know how this ends." His voice hardened like a door slamming shut in my face. "This doesn't end with freedom. This ends with war, bloodshed, and more tyranny. This won't change the world, Nic. The world will end up right back where it started. The only difference is who's on top: You."

And wouldn't I be better than them? I didn't ask the question out loud. I knew what his answer would be.

"But you can do so much more, Nic. None of this is an accident. Your giftings, the base, even the friends you're making in Beijing—it's all for such a time as this."

I finally opened my eyes and looked at him. "What do you mean?"

"You're being put in place to change the world." He cast his hand around the dome, scooping the stars up in his fingers. "But you can't do it without Him."

"Him who?"

The only clarification he offered was a sly smile. "I know He talks to you."

A rap on the door spared me the misery of acknowledging that. "Doctor?" The door creaked, and the ticket clerk peeked her head in. "We're closing soon."

"Yes, of course, thank you." My dad acknowledged her with a benevolent nod. "We'll be right down."

She shut the door and retreated. My dad turned back to the monitor and tapped a key. The viewscreen flickered off, and the telescope hummed as it settled back into its neutral position.

If only the rest of the world would put itself back where it belonged.

Dad zipped his jacket up and walked towards the door. "When can I call Cea?"

I swiveled to face him. "What? That's it?"

"Is what it? And I asked you a question."

"In June," I obliged, "and I mean—that's it? That's all you have to say?"

He glanced back at me. "Do *you* have something you want to say?"

I hesitated.

His lips twitched. "You know you can talk to your old man any time, right?" He turned and swiped his finger across the panel by the door. The dome groaned and began to shut. "Any time you want to talk, feel free to call. I'm happy to help any time—but I can't help you if you don't talk to me."

He opened the door to the hall and paused. He didn't look back, but I could hear the smile in his voice as he added, "And neither can He."

Then he walked out into the hall, leaving me alone in the loud silence.

9

"Who are you thinking about?"

I came back down to Earth with an unpleasant start and looked across the table. Min smiled at me, her face flickering in the light of the candle that tried to lend some romance to our private booth. "Who are you thinking about?" she repeated. "Because it isn't me."

"I'm sorry," I said, but didn't deny it. There was rarely any benefit in lying to Min, which was one of the reasons I liked her.

She propped her chin on her slender hand and studied me. "So? Who's the lucky girl?"

I snorted. "My dad."

Her eyes narrowed, and for a brief moment, it was as if the candle between us had gone out. "You went to see him?" Her voice held all the accusation and doubt I had been simmering in for the last hour.

"Against my better judgment," I admitted.

"What did he say?"

That I'm the next Hitler and I need to talk to Jesus more, I thought but wisely didn't say.

Enough of the truth must have made it onto my face, because she frowned. "He tried to convince you to abandon the project again, didn't he?"

I nodded, even though I was beginning to realize that was only half of it.

"And?" she prodded.

I forced my vision to focus on her again. "And what?"

"This is the part where you say 'But it didn't work, and I'm even more convinced why this project must be completed, and you have nothing to worry about, Shi Min Tai.'" She paused to refill her lungs. "Or something to that effect, but with fewer syllables."

"Good, because that's more words than I have ever used in a single sentence." I snorted, hoping we could laugh the conversation off—but she wasn't convinced.

"*Do* I have anything to worry about?"

"No," I said, but I failed to put a pause before the word.

Her whole face tightened. "Nic, please. You're scaring me."

I almost laughed. *You think you're scared? I'm abjectly terrified.* "It's fine—we just argued about Cea, that's all."

She shook her head, her dark hair dancing dangerously close to the open flame. "No, there's something more, I can tell."

I couldn't have this conversation—not with her, not here. I straightened, putting more distance between us so I could regain control of the table. "Min, I promise everything is fine. He just got on my nerves. Tell me about your work. How is—"

"No, you're going to talk to me." She grabbed my arm and tried to pull me back in, emotionally and physically. "If this is going to work between us, you need to involve me."

If what is going to work? I thought but daren't ask.

Her long fingernails kneaded my elbow. "Please, Nic. You can trust me."

I wanted to deny it. Life was so uncomplicated when you didn't trust anyone.

But I knew she was right. This woman knew things that could get me executed at the snap of a finger, and yet here we were, having dinner at the finest restaurant in Charlestown. Even if I could trust no one else on this horrid planet, I could trust her.

"I suppose you did bail me out of jail," I said, and made a payment towards my debt by offering her a genuine smile.

She accepted the sacrifice with a twinkle in her eye. "Best hundred grand I ever spent. Now tell me. What's wrong?"

I closed my eyes and tried to pull usable words out of the whirlwind. "What if… what if he's right?"

"About the project?"

"No, about me." As soon as the words left my lips, the dust began to settle.

"What about you?" Min's words were slow, stretched taut with the anxiety I was trying so hard to ignore.

I pushed her voice out of my head, for a brief minute pretending she wasn't there. I opened my eyes and stared at the candle flame, focusing on the flickering light until a vision took shape.

This is not who I am.

"Nic…?"

I turned to her. "Min, don't take this the wrong way…"

Her eyes flashed wide.

"But I don't want to be your dad."

Relief rushed back into her expression, returning the color to her cheeks. "Of course not. That's the whole reason I like you— you're not like him."

I shook my head. "No, I mean, I don't want to *be* him. I don't want his job."

"I don't follow."

I tapped my finger on my unused salad fork, rallying the courage to say the seditious words. "I don't want to be the next dictator."

She didn't respond for a long moment. When she finally spoke, her voice was painted to be reassuring, soothing. "You won't be. You could never be like him."

"I will be if I do this," I whispered, and in that moment, everything my father had ever said to me came true.

"But, Nic, you have to. There's no other way—"

"No, I don't. Min, don't you see?" I grabbed both of her hands, as if by touching her palms I could drag her into the reality that was just beyond this one. "If we do this, we start the cycle all over again. There will be another world war."

She didn't pull away, but her hands were limp in mine. "Yes, and we'll win. Someone has to be in charge, Nic. Why not us?"

Why not us? That was still the question I couldn't answer— maybe because it wasn't the one that needed to be asked.

"We can't let them win," she continued. "Think of what they've done to your parents—and it's only going to get worse. We can't let them get away with that. That's not what you're suggesting, is it?"

I shook my head. *You can't reduce this to a rhetorical question.* "No, of course not."

She wove her fingers with mine, but the gesture was slow, tentative. "Then what are you suggesting?"

The question posed there like a cliff. I knew full well that if I answered her truthfully, I would walk right off the edge—and be trusting our relationship to break my fall.

I took a deep breath and cast a thought at the one other person I knew was listening.

You'd better be right about this.

I looked into her eyes. "I think there's a better way. I think we should abandon Red Rain."

Rejection flickered across her eyes, and I died. I felt her fingers slip from mine, saw her body pull away, and felt myself falling, falling...

And then she was back, her hands tightening around mine and pulling me down to solid ground like an anchor on a ship. There was still fear in her eyes, but her voice was calm as she whispered, "I don't know what that better way is, but—I'm with you."

Air rushed back into my lungs so fast I almost choked. "Min, I—"

She put her finger to my lips. "I want you to think about it. I want you to go home, take a break. Don't touch the lab for a week. This is not the kind of decision you want to make on high… emotion."

She glanced at my empty glass, and I acknowledged the truth of that with a grunt. She was right—I was working under more than one influence tonight. But I knew the difference between the voices in my head.

"Sleep on it, then we'll talk. And if that's still what you want to do…" She pinched her eyes shut, all the doubt drawing deep lines in her face. "Then I'll support you."

"Min." I tapped her chin, forcing her to open her eyes and share in the smile I wore. "Thank you."

She cupped her hand over mine, pressing my fingers to her face. "Nic, I…" Her voice hitched on some uncomforted fear. "I need you. I can't do this without you."

"You won't have to." As the words slipped past my lips, I realized what I was saying, promising.

Her eyes searched me, the hope flickering in and out of her expression. I saw her anxiety start to crack and realized I had the power to make it all go away.

I slid my hand behind her neck, pulled her in, and kissed her.

She hesitated, her lips not moving, as if she were savoring my initiative. Then melted and kissed me back.

I gently pulled away to whisper in her ear. "I brought you something."

I let go of her to reach into the pocket of my jacket that hung on the back of my chair. My fingers closed around the object, and I hesitated.

I'd never given Min a gift before. And this was the kind of gift there was no going back from.

"You did?" she exclaimed, and the surprise in her voice was all the motivation I needed.

I pulled a jewelry box out of my pocket and turned to lay it in her hands.

She gasped, and for a second, she seemed too terrified to open it. Then she gingerly lifted the lid.

It was a single strand of pearls nestled on a bed of blue velvet.

I searched her face, but she didn't react. She stared at the gift, her face stoic.

I felt hope slip away like sand between my fingers. "Do you not like it?"

"No, no, it's beautiful." She gingerly fingered the necklace. "I just... I was hoping it was a ring."

She looked up at me and grinned, and all the sunshine came back into the room—even as tentative excitement pricked my heart.

Is that what I want?

I reached forward and slid my hand under hers. I rubbed her ring finger, imagining—wondering.

I looked back up into her eyes and smiled. "Maybe next time."

10

The call came two weeks later.

I was in the middle of dazzling a potential sponsor—the kind who would fund the base for a year if I flattered him enough—when Carnegie tapped on my elbow and held out a tablet.

I apologized to my guest and stepped away into the corner. "This better be important," I hissed, even though that was a rhetorical statement my dad would have been proud of. Carnegie only interrupted me when it was important.

"It's the government."

"I said important."

"It's about your parents."

"Maybe I better add a qualifier. This better be important *and* urgent." News about my parents, while important to me, was rarely urgent. Dad getting arrested for the second time this month didn't need my immediate attention.

Carnegie just stood there, unblinking. "It is."

I sighed to make my displeasure known, even though he was an unworthy subject, and snatched the device from him. "Stall my guests. Our paychecks are riding on this meeting."

"They always are," he said, and floated up to the table to take my place.

I hurried out of the meeting room and ducked into my office. I looked at the caller ID on the tablet, and sure enough, it was my absolute favorite people in the world: the United, Reassimilation Services Division.

I unmuted the call. "Third time's the charm."

"Excuse me?" a painfully young voice responded. "Is this Doctor—"

"Nic? Yes. And I say third time's the charm because I'm assuming you're calling me to tell me that you tried the containment camp stunt again. I hope for your sakes that it works this time."

There was a beat while the poor soul recalibrated to my sense of humor. "What containment camps, sir?"

It was said with such guileless professionalism. *This kid deserves a raise.* "Sorry, I meant 'behavioral training facility.' I forgot to turn on my bureaucratic filter." I walked over and flipped on the coffee maker. If I was going to have to deal with the government, I needed a fresh pot.

"I'm not sure what you're referring to, sir." The kid cleared his throat in a vain attempt to regain control of the conversation. "I called to tell you that you're needed back on Earth."

In his defense, that was a new one. "Why?"

"We believe they will be much more responsive to treatment if administered by a trusted face—"

"Whoa," I cut him off. "Hang on."

"What?"

I ignored him, yanked the cup off the coffee maker, and took a swig, ignoring the dribble on the tray as the machine continued to dispense. I set the cup back on the machine and cleared my throat. "I'm going to need you to try again. I don't know what that stupid script they gave you says, but I'm pretty sure you're not supposed to lead with that."

"Actually, sir, that's exactly what it says…"

"Then rewrite it. What do you mean, 'treatment'? What sort of moronic pseudoscience are you trying on my poor folks now?"

He went silent, and my blood ran cold.

Once again, my careless words had been prophetic. And once again, I would have given anything to be proven wrong.

The kid still hadn't found his courage, so I decided to help him out. I sat down at the desk and opened a note file. "Start from the beginning."

He did. My parents had been put on trial again—the usual song and dance—and this time, the judge had risked recommission to issue a severe sentence: neurosurgery.

It was an unpopular corrective device, even for dealing with thorns in the flesh like my dad. It wasn't that it didn't work; if the intent was to force patients to forget about their religion, national identity, and other pesky idiosyncrasies that prevented assimilation, then the treatment had a perfect success rate.

The problem was that patients often also died. And while the United was not against executing people, there were far cheaper ways to do it. Even the government wasn't *that* grossly inefficient.

By some miracle, both of my parents had survived. But the more the kid described their condition, the more I realized their survival may not have been a mercy.

The kid claimed they had forgotten everything they knew, including the majority of their life and social skills. He described their condition as that of a two-year-old.

"The doctors believe that, with consistent therapy, they will be able to—"

"Show me," I demanded.

"What?"

I gripped the desk with both hands, forcing myself to say the words I knew would end in disaster. "I want to see them."

"Now?"

"No, I have an opening next Tuesday. Of course now!" My voice rose to a shout, my whole body lurching with the effort. The desk rocked.

"I—I suppose I can patch you into the hospital."

"Please do."

It took him a good ten minutes—during which I asked to see his manager twice—but he managed to call the facility and get their doctor on the line. The doctor tried to give me the same spiel, just embellished with more technical terms, but I didn't give him the grace. After I issued several veiled and unveiled threats, he finally enabled a video call and let me see my father.

Dad looked fine, which was the most disturbing thing about the whole ordeal. There was no scarring, no bandage, no stitches; neurosurgery was a completely nano-driven procedure. He was alert and seemed to be in perfect health.

But he looked so confused.

"What's that?" he asked, voice several pitches too high. He pointed at the tablet some nurse was shakily holding up to his face.

I turned on my camera. "Paul."

His head jerked around, as if he couldn't figure out where the sound was coming from. "Who's Paul?"

"That's you, remember?" the nurse offered oh-so-sweetly.

But he didn't. He clearly didn't.

I don't know why I said it. I knew what was going to happen, the disappointment I was inviting on myself. But I had to do it. I had to try one last time.

"Dad," I said, and I repeated the word until his eyes focused on me. I leaned towards the camera, as if that could span the millions of miles between us. "Dad, it's me."

His response was immediate. "Who are you?"

I ended the video.

The underpaid clerk was still waiting on the other line. "I know this is a lot to take in, sir."

Can't even bend your bureaucracy to apologize, can you? I sank back in the chair, letting my muscles melt like plastic dissolved by acid.

"But you're needed back on Earth immediately."

"Why?" *I'm never going back. You can keep your stupid planet.*

"You need to assist with administrating the therapy. They will need round-the-clock observation, and we believe their chances of success increase with…"

I laughed, the sound as painful as broken glass. "Absolutely not. I'm current on my taxes."

"Sir?"

"Government healthcare includes end-of-life care, does it not?"

"Y-yes, for fully assimilated citizens—"

The truth sank into me like a knife. "Which they are now."

He couldn't deny it. "The government wants—"

"The government got what it wanted. Now it can clean up the mess." I didn't give him a chance to counter that, if he was even intelligent enough to do so. "I want daily reports on their progress and access to their full medical files."

"Sir, I'm not authorized to—"

"You're not? No worries, I know someone who is. Surname is Mong."

I would never have bothered Min with something as paltry as this, but I knew I wouldn't have to. The clerk's stuttering reached a new pitch. "Mong? Of-of course, sir, I'll set that up right away."

I hung up without thanking him.

I shoved my chair back and stormed over to the coffee maker. I grabbed my mug, stopped, and stared.

The dark liquid rippled as my hand shook. My whole body— my arms, my legs, my mind, my universe—was shaking. And there was no gravitational pull that could put my world back in orbit.

All this—the base, Red Rain, the coup—was to protect my family. It was to save my parents, save Cea, save me, save everyone who looked and thought and talked differently. We were going to crumble the United so that we would never have to suffer their injustices again.

But I was too late. Red Rain was a failure.

I was a failure.

I screamed. The primal yell rasped against my throat and agitated the darkness that descended on my mind like a dust storm. I turned and hurled my mug into the wall, relishing the chaos as the ceramic shattered and the coffee splattered.

Something shoved its way up my throat. I fought it, tried to swallow it like unwelcome bile, but it flared into an urge I could not deny. What point was there in resisting? There was no point in fighting. Not anymore.

So I surrendered, collapsed against the wall, and wept.

✷

The nightmares returned immediately.

Of course, I only slept a combined four hours over the next three days. It took twenty-four hours of vicious phone calls and blackmailing before I was finally granted full access to my parents' medical files. I spent the next forty-eight scouring the data, trying to figure out who had done this.

The court case had been completely classified. Even my black-market connections couldn't hack in. I could find absolutely no explanation as to who had charged my parents or even what they had been charged with. I scoured my parents' personnel files trying to figure out what they had done to anger the law, but they had been unusually compliant over the last several months. I could not find any reason why even the pedantic United would justify the procedure.

Why them? And why now? They'd done nothing—nothing out of the ordinary—and Dad was still on their payroll. He'd had enough of his rights stripped away over the years that he was little better than an indentured servant, but he was still their best scientist. From his government-monitored lab in Boston, he was doing more to advance the colonies on Mars than all the students at Stanford combined.

Or at least he had been, before they'd used a nanobot to rewrite his brain circuitry.

I turned to their medical files next. I researched the neurologist, the surgeon, the director of the hospital—even their anesthesiologist. I couldn't find anything suspicious in their records, no prejudice or bias or history of malpractice. None of them were even running for office. They had absolutely nothing to gain from the procedure. As near as the record showed, they had simply been hired to do a job.

And then, finally, I found who had hired them.

Deep within the recesses of Dad's medical history, I found a digital signature. Neurosurgery was a highly restricted procedure, and it required multiple layers of government approval. Most of the permission slips had been classified, but there are always redundancies with computer records. And in this case, they'd forgotten that the lab also had a copy of the release for the special anesthesia.

I decrypted the file, and a government ID popped up on the screen:

MONG SHI MIN TAI

I panicked, my heart and brain flying into survival mode like I was being held at gunpoint. Everything in me willed the universe to conjure up another explanation, some logic that would reconcile this information with the truth I needed.

I grabbed my phone. Min and I had spoken little over the past few days. Correction: *I* had spoken little. I'd told her the news, inciting a barrage of texts and calls from her that I did not return. She had expressed her sympathy repeatedly and offered her assistance—financial and physical.

I scrolled to the bottom of our message history, to the text she had sent a mere hour ago:

THIS IS WHY WE NEED RED RAIN

Suddenly, everything made sense.

The world flashed black and white, and in that split moment of pure rage, I considered calling her. But to what end? So she could snivel and beg and try to convince me that this was all for my own good? I didn't have time for that. So I blocked her on every platform and device and hoped she would take the hint.

She didn't.

Three weeks later, she showed up at the base. I was in the lab, buried in a pointless experiment designed to distract my mind from bigger problems, when Carnegie interrupted me.

"I have a docking request, sir, but I have no arrivals on the agenda."

I held two vials up to the light. I poured one into the other, not because I needed the compound, but because I had to see the color change, the molecules move, the liquid slide against the glass—anything to fill the void that had become my subconscious. "Who is it?"

"That's just it—the vehicle registration is classified."

I slammed the empty vial down on the table, shattering it.

"Doctor?"

I brushed the glass shards into a pile. "The only people allowed to classify information is the government, Carnegie. Tell her to leave."

He was being unusually slow. "Her?"

I didn't elaborate. "The docking request has been denied."

After a flicker of hesitation, Carnegie lifted the tablet he carried and keyed my command onto the screen. I crossed my arms and waited.

As I suspected, she didn't take no for an answer. Carnegie turned the tablet to face me. "They're requesting to speak to you."

"Regrettably for them, I'm booked solid."

"They're sending over ID... It's Min." The tablet chirped. "Correction, she's *ordering* you to speak to her."

I cackled. "She of all people should know I'm terrible at following orders."

Carnegie's eyes flickered. He probably would have gone pale had there been any shades between him and copy paper. Unlike me, Carnegie still had a healthy fear of Min's influence. "Do I need to remind you that she can have you defunded in about five minutes?"

"It would probably take her closer to ten with the signal delay, but no, you don't. I just don't care."

Carnegie frowned. "Well, I do." He punched the button to enable audio and held the tablet out to me.

I grunted a choice word. "You're fired," I snarled, and snatched the tablet from him.

"Nic," Min's voice crackled over the speaker.

I leaned against the table and waited.

"Nic," she repeated. "Nic? Talk to me. Please."

Carnegie arched an eyebrow. I picked at my teeth.

Min huffed, her breath rippling the line. "Nic Joseph Von Nieuwen—"

I grimaced. "If you're wondering how long I can sit here and let you babble into an empty line, the answer is *all* day. I'll even clear my afternoon."

"Nic." She breathed again, a relieved sound this time. "Please, let's talk about this. I can explain."

"Babe," I said with enough sucrose to rot a tooth. "You don't have to explain anything."

Her desperation must have made her deaf, because she fell for it. "I don't?"

"No, of course not." I let my benevolence hang for a moment before dropping the knife. "I know exactly what you did and why you did it."

"But I—"

"They were unnecessary, weren't they?" My pain leeched into my voice, making it sharp like vinegar and salt. "My parents were an unnecessary mess that you just *had* to clean up."

She hesitated a beat too long. "Nic, I'm sorry, I—"

"No need to apologize. I'm the one who fell for it—for you." I picked up a vial and tossed it in my palm. "It's a shame, really. If I hadn't hacked into the medical records... it might have worked."

I thought of the necklace and the kiss and the candlelit dates and realized just how true that was.

"Nic, please," she begged, and the impending tears were genuine. "I need you."

I laughed—long, cold, and hard. "Don't lie to me."

"But I'm not—"

"You don't *need* me. You have a copy of the research. Find another scientist."

Carnegie shifted.

Min had the manners to process that before replying. "You're right," she said, and took a deep breath. "I don't need you."

I pressed the vial to my lips, closed my eyes, and waited.

"But I want you."

I opened my eyes and stood up. "Regrettably, *Asia*..." I let the name close the lid on the coffin, "...I don't want you."

I ended the call.

I held the tablet out to Carnegie. It took an inordinate amount of time for him to gather his wits and take it. "Is your will drawn up, doctor?"

"What?" I barked, suddenly feeling very tired.

He swiped on the screen. "Because I think you just signed your own death warrant."

I spat another laugh. "One can only hope." If Asia wanted to put me out of my misery, let her. But I knew she wouldn't. Love was a cruel master, and in this case, it would work in my favor.

The tablet screeched. "She's still requesting to dock."

I sighed and turned back to my workstation. "Carnegie, what *do* I pay you for? Take care of it."

He hesitated, craggily finger posed over the screen. I saw the cowardly fear dance in his eyes and wondered if he was about to defect—and then, suddenly, his emotion evaporated. "Of course, sir." He spun and strode from the room.

I waited until the door had slid shut behind him before sagging against the table. In some sick way, it wasn't Asia's deception that bothered me. I had done the same to other people in the process of securing sponsorships. That was how the game was played—I went into these relationships expecting to use and be used.

I did not go into them expecting to fall in love.

I couldn't decide whether to vomit or flip the table. Since grief was a highly unpleasant emotion to process, I chose the latter.

I roared and swiped my arm across the table, scattering the instruments. A welcome symphony of destruction erupted as metal clattered and glass shattered. Spilled chemicals bled together, adding an accompaniment of fizzles and steam.

I watched as the contents of two overturned flasks pooled on the table. A stream of yellow hastened to marry a puddle of orange, and when they kissed, they turned to blood. The newly forged acid trickled over the side of the table, where it instantly scarred the linoleum.

I watched the caustic chemical eat away at the floor and, for the first time since my visit to Earth, regretted stopping the Red Rain project. It would be nice to watch the world burn.

The door hissed open. "I've taken care of—doctor!"

Carnegie grabbed a spill kit off the wall and darted over, but I put up my hand. "Wait."

"Sir?"

I watched as the stream dried to a trickle. *What if...*

I strode to the other side of the room, where a whiteboard was shoved in the corner. I dragged it out and spun it around.

My incomplete formula for Red Rain was still written on the surface in mismatched colors, right where I'd abandoned it a month ago. I traced the imperfect chemical equation with my eyes, compounding, simulating—imagining.

"It's too subtle," I thought aloud.

"Sir?"

"Red Rain. It's too subtle. Too localized. It's limited to how far and fast a plane can spread it—and they could always shoot the plane down. It would never win in a large-scale attack."

"Are you planning a large-scale attack?"

I didn't answer. I grabbed a marker and tossed the cap on the floor. Then I started scribbling on the whiteboard. "But what if it really is raining?"

Carnegie came to stand by my elbow. "Explain."

"It's all in the name—Red Rain. We make it an environmental weapon." I had no idea what the chemical compound would look like yet, so I tried to emphasize with pictures and a diagram. "I don't know how we'll distribute it—gas, probably—but what if we could contaminate the air? What if we could release this compound into the environment, and as soon as it started raining, it would turn into acid?"

"Sir," Carnegie said again, this time with admiration.

"You could decimate an entire city—country—and no one would be able to stop it." I threw the marker on the tray and paused, for one final moment appreciating what I was saying. "We could win any war."

Carnegie folded his arms, his winkled hands disappearing in the folds of his lab coat. "May I ask, doctor... is there a war you'd like to win?"

I knew what he was asking, challenging.

We both know how this ends.

I dragged my finger across the whiteboard, smearing part of the equation. "My dad was right about one thing."

Carnegie frowned but waited.

I looked up at the ceiling, where a flicker of the Martian sky shone through the windows. "I am no better than they are."

2076
PRESENT DAY

11

I waited until the memories had run their course and slunk back into the recesses of my mind. As soon as the relative silence returned, I reached up and stroked my fingers across the keypad next to the door.

The room shuddered and moaned as the ceiling began to part. The panels folded in on themselves, revealing a seamless dome of glass. Mars' dim moons lent barely any light, but it was just enough for me to make out the shape of the telescope in the middle of the room.

She stood idle, her frame covered in dust and her mirrors still wrapped in protective film. I had almost finished building her when I got the news about my parents' neurosurgery. Out of defiance and hope, I completed the project. It took two years—two years of watching my parents go through humiliating therapy—before I acknowledged that it was a wasted effort.

The telescope had never seen first light. And she never would.

*

The invitation was late this year.

It usually came in March, several months in advance of the event, as was proper with a formal invitation. This year, the envelope didn't arrive until the middle of July—much too late for me to reasonably plan a trip to Earth, not that I had any intention of attending.

Had she forgotten? Had I finally been released from the prison of her memory? I squinted at the ornate United postmark. She had only mailed the invite two weeks ago and expedited it by private transit.

Overcompensating, as always.

I opened my lower desk drawer and prepared to add the envelope to my collection. For eight years she had been inviting me, and for eight years she had written the same message on the back of the envelope. For eight years I had allowed silence to be my RSVP.

And yet, for some reason—perhaps the same one that prevented me from demolishing the observatory I had built for Dad—I couldn't bring myself to throw the invitations away. So they sat, unopened, in chronological order, at the back of the drawer.

I flipped the envelope over and bent to file it—and froze.

She'd written a different note this year. She'd used a new color of ink and made the cursive letters larger and curlier so that I would be sure to notice. How kind of her—it would have been a shame if I had missed the carefully-articulated threat.

YOU REALLY MUST COME. AFTER ALL, IT'S ANDROMEDA'S BIRTHDAY –MIN

TO BE CONTINUED...

GET A FREE PREQUEL!

Sign up for my newsletter and download *Project 74* for free! Plus, as a subscriber, you'll be the first to know about new releases, get sneak peeks of upcoming books, and more!

Sign up at:
rachelnewhouse.com/subscribe

WANT EXCLUSIVE BONUS SCENES?

Become a Patron and get access to **exclusive bonus scenes** for this series! Plus, you can get digital ARCs, collector's edition hardbacks, and merch, or read my WIP as I write it!

Become a Patron at:
patreon.com/rachelnewhouse

DID YOU LOVE THIS BOOK?

Please consider leaving a review on Amazon or
Goodreads! It's one of the most important things you
can do to support an indie author. Thank you!

HI FROM RACHEL

Rachel Newhouse is an author, wife, secretary, and Sunday school teacher from Kansas City, Missouri. Her obsessions are sci-fi, dystopian, and kid lit. When she's not writing, she's cooking Asian food, growing chilis that are too spicy to eat, and watching wildly age-inappropriate shows like *My Little Pony* and *Gravity Falls* with her husband, Joe. She also really likes glitter. You've been warned.

Connect with Rachel:
bio.site/rachelnewhouse